The Rage of Trograin

. . . His lips brushed her face, her neck, her hair, and she longed for him to kiss her. Instead, he tantalized her with his whispering and the gentle exploration of his mouth . . .

"Oh, Tom," she cried.

But it was not Tom.

Coldness filled the room like a blast of wind off a glacier. The form in her arms turned to ice. Terror set in so intensely that she could not move, yet she knew if it did not release her she would die. She struggled feebly, a scream frozen in her throat . . .

An Ancient Rage

by
Jacqueline La Tourrette

A DELL BOOK

"Of a stone, a leaf, an unfound door,
and all the forgotten places . . ."
Thomas Wolfe

Published by
Dell Publishing Co., Inc.
1 Dag Hammarskjold Plaza
New York, New York 10017

Copyright © 1978 by Jacqueline Gibeson

All rights reserved. No part of this book may be reproduced or transmitted in any form or by any means, electronic or mechanical, including photocopying, recording or by any information storage and retrieval system, without the written permission of the Publisher, except where permitted by law.

Dell ® TM 681510, Dell Publishing Co., Inc.

ISBN: 0-440-19060-6

Printed in the United States of America

First printing—December 1978

PROLOGUE

He moved in his slumber. Soon, now . . . soon. Something broke his sleep and he listened, all senses alert, as once he had done in the green forest hunting. The harsh cadence of their speech was unfamiliar; they were still here, and his hatred grew faster than hope, until he almost had to suppress a cry. One there was who understood him, but it was difficult to get through. Many had passed, disturbing his rest during his long confinement, but none had been strong enough to free him, except at one time of the year when he was strongest.

The invisible door was almost impassable and, in the mold of perpetual darkness, he waited.

CHAPTER ONE

THE GUEST HOUSE stood on the tip of a hill overlooking the sea a few miles south of Dublin, a half-timber structure with jutting eaves and a modest English garden. Barely visible from the road below, it had the quaint Alpine name, the Chalet. The hill was green the year around and high enough not to be swallowed by the morning mists from the water, commanding an unmatched view of the point, adjoining the grounds of what must have been a mansion in the old Anglo-Irish days. Its more imposing neighbor, Corrig, had fallen into disrepair and abandonment now, due to the prohibitive cost of its upkeep. The crenelations of Corrig's tower grimaced like broken teeth above its beard of ivy; its windows had been broken by the stones of village boys. It was like a small, angry castle at sunset, when the red glow from the water struck the remaining glass in the turret. It looked like a haunted house.

The guest house, on the other hand, has fared better. On the surface, there is nothing sinister there. It has maintained its dignity and can afford to be serene. Purchased ten years ago with a small down payment by a widowed nurse, it was a rest home for a while, until Mrs. Coghan found the location unfavorable for the purpose. Her patients would get sick, they would even die, and it was almost impossible to maneuver the hill with a stretcher. The path rambled between trees and rocks, turning sharply and breaking into stone steps along the way. Finally, after a corpse and bearers took a grotesque tumble on the misty steps one morning, she was forced into a decision that changed her whole life. She turned the Chalet into a guest house for people who were on holiday in Ireland, and the same guests came and went over the years and returned again, which had never happened in her nursing. They wrote letters from England and America, as though the Chalet were their second home. There were the other kind of guests, too, of course, and Mrs. Coghan had never figured them out: the ones who paid a fortnight in advance and did not remain after one night in the house. There was an alikeness about them she had come to recognize: a tension, a quiet awareness. They complained of noises in the night and became subtly disturbed by the pleasant surroundings. When they left, she was relieved to see them go.

There was one of these people in the house now, but he did not leave. He seemed to be enjoying himself immensely. She almost wished he would go. Mr. Hughes had stayed for six months, now: she was not sure if he was a guest or another patient. She suspected a heart condition and, again, the path worried her. He might die up here like the others and have to be carried down on a stretcher. The worst of it was that despite his peculiarities she had grown fond of the old man. He was friendly and neat. He paid regularly and he had a very witty tongue. He filled a need in her. She missed her nursing, despite her constant ministrations to her aged mother, and she looked after Mr. Hughes without fuss but with a constant alertness of which he was quite unaware.

He was like the others, though. He had that quiet expectation like an animal hearing what others do not. He smiled to himself sometimes as he sat by the fire, looking up occasionally to see if the other guests had heard it, too. The night before he had really upset her.

After the other guests had gone to bed, she went over to clean his ashtray. He grinned up at her through his beard. "What do you know about your house, Mrs. Coghan? Who owned it before you?"

"I bought it from old Mrs. Langen," she said, dumping the tobacco and ashes into the hearth. "She wanted to go to England to live with her daughter. She lived here all her married life."

"Who had it before she did?"

"I don't think she told me. The house is over a hundred years old. It's in good condition, though, except for the plumbing. A makeshift job that is. It's always breaking down."

He was silent a moment; he seemed to be

amused. "Tell me the truth about that stone in the garden," he said, cupping his hand over his pipe to light it.

"Sure we've been over that before! It's a stone, that's all. The monks must have put it there. Who's to know what monks mean anyway?"

He chuckled softly and his laugh had a comforting sound. "Indeed, who's to know?" he said, imitating her accent. "The place was never a monastery, Mrs. Coghan. The grounds may have been connected with one, but the only large house around here is Corrig. It's not a monastery and never was. It was obviously a fine private residence."

"Well, they tore the monastery down, then. What difference does it make?"

"The stone's no older than Corrig," he said thoughtfully. "I can tell by the engraving. A hundred and fifty, maybe two hundred years. No, the stone wasn't there before Corrig was built. Where's your Irish imagination, woman? Don't you want to know about the past? Who lived here . . . and what happened to them? Your grounds must have been part of Corrig. Who built the Chalet, then . . . and why? And, most of all, who erected that stone? That fantastic stone."

"I've trouble enough in the present without worrying about the past," she said, beginning to grow uneasy. These were the same questions that the man who threw the fit had asked. "It doesn't concern me at all."

His red-brown eyes narrowed slightly and he

smiled. "You're a good practical woman, Mrs. Coghan, but you're suppressing something from me." He sighed, and almost to himself, he said, "Your house is a little haunted, you know."

She was so unnerved that she went right to the gin bottle in her room. She did not drink often, but it was a comfort, and there was no harm in it at her time of life. It relaxed her a little, and nothing but the increased flush on her face revealed that she did it. The day girls never had to do her work. But she drank two tumblers after talking to Mr. Hughes.

For the first time, it had been put into words, and everything in her rebelled against the assumption. Some of her old patients had said things; her mother was a listener, too. She hoped that her mother did not get hold of Mr. Hughes's story . . . it might set her off again. Mrs. Coghan did not believe in ghosts: she could not afford to. The Chalet was her home and it was a far finer house than she had ever dreamed of owning when she was young enough to dream. It was congenial, well ordered. The routine was so smooth she had time to watch the portable television in the parlor, which could be moved to her own quarters when the guests were out. The house had done well by her. Her sons were being properly educated at a moderately priced parochial boarding school and her mother was being cared for in her old age. Still, the warnings made her feel uneasy, and she poured another half tumbler of gin. She felt guilty, somehow, as though she were misrepresenting her house. Only a few people had reacted badly to it but, then, she remembered old Mrs. Ryan.

The old lady, who had been one of her patients, could not be considered senile. Though she was eighty-five, her little eyes were bright and alert. She came from the islands and spoke Gaelic, which hardly anyone her age did in Dublin, under English rule. The language had not been revived until the revolution of 1922. The old woman, too, had been fascinated by the stone in the garden: she used to prod the moss on it with her walking stick. In fact she seemed in every way to be making an investigation of the premises, and she asked a lot of questions, too. It was wet November when they found her in the back garden near the turf shed. She had lain dead in the rain all night. She was the first one who mentioned any strangeness about the place to Mrs. Coghan. And now Mr. Hughes was up to same thing.

A stiff prescription of gin in the morning made her forget uncertainties of the previous night. She was happy again now as she cleaned the parlor in expectation of a new guest. The old man sat at his usual place by the fire, dozing with an open book in his lap. He looked pale today: he kept such unusual hours. She was moved by affection for him as she cleaned the table at his elbow. She knew she could not ask him to leave. He had not spoken of family, but she was sure he was alone. He had not had any post since he came here. Such a solitary and independent old man had obviously cared for himself for a long time. She gave the table a final lemon-scented polish and sighed.

The new young lady would be here soon. Her room was ready with the extra table she had requested, and the tea kettle was on the stove. Upstairs, Miss Fay and her niece were settling in after their shopping trip to Dublin. Their voices and the rattle of paper indicated the success of the expedition. It was nice to have Miss Fay back, even with that niece she brought along with her this time. It was shocking the way the girl dressed: she looked like something from a spaceship. And she was a very moody girl. A bit taken with herself, Mrs. Coghan thought. She had explained rather unpleasantly that the clothes she wore were the fashion in England, but Mrs. Coghan could not believe it. She did not connect the television in any way with life. She must ask Mr. Jamieson about it. He was an Englishman. He was a dear man, and she felt comfortable with him. A little out of place here and too solitary, though. Obviously well-educated, he was not snobbish, as some in her experience had been. Mr. Jamieson, she felt, had a problem, but she was not going to get it out of him. He took long walks alone, and was probably doing so this afternoon.

Mrs. Coghan was a little tired and her feet ached. She sat down in one of the flower-patterned chairs and surveyed the domain of her parlor. The gin had relaxed the tension she had felt earlier in the day. Sunlight streamed through the half-opened drapes and glinted on the Indian brass table she had picked up at an auction for five pounds. One of the maids had placed a bowl of chrysanthemums in the indentation in the middle, and she was vaguely appreciative of the effect. It was a lovely room altogether, she thought. Then she began to concern herself with tea. She would never be upset or apologetic about her house: she need not feel any guilt at all.

The doorbell chimed. Mr. Hughes snorted in his chair and opened his eyes, retrieving at once his dignity and his book. Mrs. Coghan opened the flowered drapes to admit more sunlight, with another brief glance over her parlor. The brass coffee table gleamed and every chair cover was smooth, but something seemed to be out of place. When her gaze reached the fireplace, she knew what it was. The first person Miss Rudloe would meet would be the old man. She paused uncertainly before going to the door.

Without looking up from his book, Mr. Hughes raised his hand and said, "Not a word, Mrs. Coghan, I swear it. I've no intention of frightening your guests."

The bell chimed again, more insistently, and he chuckled as she rushed to answer it, the color high in her face. Miss Rudloe was leaning against the porch railing, loaded down with her luggage and books, a yellow scarf askew on her dark hair, and there was perspiration on her forehead. She smiled quickly when the door at last produced Mrs. Coghan.

"I've had the most awful time finding this place," she said. "I took a wrong turn on the path and dropped my typewriter and wound up at the eeriest looking old house you ever saw." She indicated the direction she had come from while Mrs. Coghan helped her with her things. "What is that place anyhow? The local 'most haunted' house?"

Mrs. Coghan tensed and looked over her shoulder into the room. When she answered, she lowered her voice so Mr. Hughes would not hear her. "It's Corrig, my dear. It isn't haunted at all; it has no one to look after it anymore." Then her voice resumed its normal pitch. "God love you, you should have left your things down at the gate! Come in, come in! Put your books on the window seat. There's a coatrack behind you at the foot of the stairs. Mary!" she called. "Mary! You're just in time for tea; the others will be down soon. Mary! That girl's never around when I need her. She has anemia and has to have iron injections. If it doesn't kill her soon, I will. How did you get here from Dublin? Not by bus, I hope. Mary, come here at once, do you hear?"

Bewildered by the tidal wave of questions and observations crashing against her ears, Monica Rudloe merely smiled and shook her head as she struggled out of her coat. She smoothed her hair with her hand and looked into the parlor. It was as warm and comfortable as she remembered it from last week when she came to engage her room. The sight of it was comforting after her hike on the hill.

"I thought I'd exaggerated it in my mind," she smiled. "It's so much what I wanted. But it's everything I remembered and more. . . ."

The old man sitting by the fireplace cleared his throat and Monica smiled at him. The room would have been somehow incomplete without him, though she had not seen him when she was here before. She took a step toward him, but was checked by Mrs. Coghan's hand on her arm.

"You'll want to go to your room to tidy up before tea. I'll get Mary to carry your things. She must be in the back somewhere."

Monica wanted to say she would carry them herself. She did not want someone deathly ill hauling her luggage for her. But Mrs. Coghan disappeared through a doorway and the old man cleared his throat again. He rose from his chair. He might have been in his mid-sixties and he wore an old brown tweed suit, complete with vest, which matched his graying chestnut beard and fox-colored eyes. His clothing hung on him and covered his body loosely as though he had lost weight since it was tailored. A crescent smile tipped with gold flashed in his beard.

"Miss Rudloe? Mrs. Coghan's been awaiting you on tenterhooks. I can see why now. She likes Americans, you know. Don't worry about the maid. Her anemia's merely functional. It gets her a day's sick leave once a month."

It was as though he had read her mind. She extended her hand and clutched his tightly, feeling a little tense and unsteady on her feet. The pressure of his old fingers made her nerves vibrate to the point of almost screaming, and she withdrew her hand quickly and sank down in a chair. "What on earth are tenterhooks?" she asked lightly, but her voice broke. It had come on so quickly, perhaps from her climb up the hill. She should have had lunch while she was packing in Dublin. It would look queer if she fainted over tea. She looked up at the old man again and he was studying her.

"You're Welsh," she said rather surprisingly, and he laughed outright.

"I was . . . many years ago. Oxford took it out of me. A life term at an English boys' school made me forget the rest. As for tenterhooks, my dear young lady, I think we're in trouble. I thought it was an American word. No? Well, we need a dictionary then. Surprising how many words we use with no idea of their meaning. Take 'Adam's off-ox' for example. I thought it was something rude until I finally looked it up."

The giddiness receded while he was talking, but now everything came too sharply into focus. Every hair in his beard stood out in neat precision like a microphotograph, and the flowers on the chair cover shouted up at her with the angry tongues of their printed pistils. She ran her hand across her forehead. What did psychologists call it, this heightened perception and dimming of personal identity? She knew it had a name, but she could not think of it.

"My name's Hughes," the old man was saying. "Evan Hughes. Perhaps Mrs. Coghan told you?"

Monica shook her head and his eyes glinted. "You informed me I was Welsh, then, before you heard it."

"You're a teacher, too?" she asked quickly to change the subject. Depersonalization, was that it? Nothing like this had ever happened before. "I instruct in a girls' college back home."

"I'm retired, thank God! I don't have to face the little bastards anymore. Mr. Chips was sick, you know."

She laughed suddenly, liking the old man immensely, and everything was all right again. She relaxed against the back of her chair to appraise him and his eyes twinkled back at her.

"My girls are all right, really," she smiled. "Girls take naturally to literature because they're basically romantic. Some of them even like Joyce, though. They frighten me a little."

He tamped tobacco into his pipe thoughtfully. "Straight hair, glasses," he outlined in a kind of verbal shorthand, "the eagerly intellectual stare. Yes. They crowd around your desk after class, don't they? They want to know more about Molly Bloom, but they use the mask of Penelope to cover it. 'Miss Rudloe, I can't get the skeleton key to *Finnegans Wake* in the library . . . may I borrow yours?'" He chuckled to himself and Moncia straightened in her chair.

"What *are* you?" she asked unsteadily, but he cleared his throat and ignored the question.

"Do you like Joyce?" he asked.

"I'm stuck with him," she said, still watching

the old man closely. "I'm here to write my thesis. 'The Influence of the Church on Modern Irish Writers.' I'm not doing very well."

"It's because you aren't a Catholic. Why didn't you like your quarters in Dublin?"

She shook her head. "Everyone was too friendly. My lord, how the Irish can talk! And I couldn't stop listening. When I finally got time alone, I got so engrossed in my paper, I forgot to eat. I had to get away," she smiled, "to get some work done without starving."

His foxy eyes burned and the gold crown flashed in his mouth. "It's like being tuned in between radio stations, isn't it? Picking up several programs and police calls at the same time. You can turn a radio off, but you have to run away when it happens in your life."

Monica fell silent. The sounds of voices and cutlery could be heard in the next room. She felt too exhausted to go in to tea. "You ran away, didn't you?" she said quietly, and made a startled gesture with her hand. "I'm sorry! I don't know what made me say that."

He did not attempt to hold back the excitement in his voice. "But it's happened before, hasn't it? Oh, Miss Rudloe, you're just what I need!" He noticed her sudden withdrawal and tried to control himself. "You're right, of course. I did run away. They were smothering me into an early grave. My son and his wife. Nice people, really, but not my sort." He gave a wheezy little laugh. "I have letters posted from all over Eurpoe . . . without return addresses. It's a marvelous arrangement. It keeps my conscience clear. Let's see. . . . this week I'm in Rome, I think."

She could not suppress her laugh. "Mr. Hughes, that's a dreadful thing to do!"

"Yes, isn't it? But I didn't know how else to handle the situation without hurting their feelings. They're very dutiful. They're also very square. You won't tell anyone?"

"Of course not; why should I? You're a grown man . . . I think."

Their gazes met and held, a flow of silent amusement passed between them.

"We're going to be more than friends," the old man said. "However, Miss Fay and her niece are about to descend the staircase for tea. I'll talk to you later. You'll like Miss Fay; I do. One of the most innocent hearts I've ever known. A lady born . . . as rare as an insect in amber these days. You'll just have to put up with her niece."

Monica glanced toward the staircase just as a pair of shapely magenta legs topped by a short green skirt descended. Her reaction made Mr. Hughes wheeze with delight. The girl was followed immediately by a delicate little lady in a white lace blouse who smiled as she extended her hand.

"Mr. Hughes," she said as he rose to greet her. "We've had the most delightful day! We went mad-out-of-our-minds and bought everything! Lynette found the loveliest Aran knit, didn't you, dear?"

The girl shrugged sullenly and stared at Monica from under the bangs covering her eyebrows. She was sixteen or seventeen, heavily made up, with magnificent eyes, but there was no youth about her. Monica switched her attention to the aunt, who seemed to have the premium of youth in the family.

"I'm Monica Rudloe," she introduced herself with a handshake betraying her nationality. "I think Mr. Hughes is taken with you."

Miss Fay colored to her pale hairline and looked charmingly flustered. She was a pretty woman in her mid-fifties with a fair English complexion and startling blue eyes. "I'm glad you're here," she said sincerely. "This is my niece, Lynette. It hasn't been much of a holiday for her. No one near her own age, you know. I so wanted to show her this place: I was born in the village. But I hadn't considered how she would spend her time. Now she'll have someone to talk to. Children her age love Americans, you know."

Monica nodded at the girl. "You have a very romantic name. Right out of Tennyson." The girl's face registered scorn so she quickly changed her tactics. "I think I'll just call you Lyn."

The girl's love of Americans was not evident. She gave Monica a supercilious glance and turned away with that irritating shrug again, as if to say, "It's no concern of mine what you call me!" Monica thought of a better name. This was a type she knew well: the most difficult student to reach, completely wrapped up in her own adolescence.

She decided not to force herself on the girl. She was here to work on her paper, not to get involved with the other guests.

"Shall we go in for tea?" Miss Fay asked timidly. "Mr. Jamieson isn't here yet."

"He'll be along in a moment." Mr. Hughes took the lady's arm and Monica and Lyn followed the old couple into the dining room.

The table was generously laid with fresh buttered bread, hot scones, and jam. Monica decided her earlier giddiness had been due to malnutrition and did not eat with restraint. The maid was pouring her second cup of tea when a tall man in a sweater and slacks entered the room with mumbled apologies and took his place beside her. His gray-blond hair was disordered by the wind, his gray eyes abstracted in a craggily handsome face. When Mr. Hughes introduced them, he seemed to dismiss her at once from his mind, and drank his tea in silence, as though he were alone in the room. Instead of making her uncomfortable, Monica found Mr. Jamieson's attitude soothing. She had already met too many people today. She was tired to the bone and wanted only to escape to her room to rest. She was a little startled when Lyn spoke out boldly to the reticent gentleman.

"Where have you been all afternoon?" the girl asked in a remarkably cultivated English voice. "I looked for you on the beach from my window, but you weren't there."

He looked up from his plate wearily, focusing his attention with difficulty, but when he did, he smiled at her. "I didn't follow my usual pattern. I took a hike up the hill across the road instead."

He addressed the girl in a very friendly way, treating her as an equal instead of the unpleasant child she was, and his manner drew a longer look from Monica. He was old enough to be Lyn's father, so it was not anything romantic. Perhaps he had a daughter of his own, the way he talked to her. He did not want to talk; he had something on his mind. But he made a special effort to communicate with the girl.

"What did you do today?" he asked. "I haven't seen you since breakfast. It was so quiet without your radio blaring, I thought you might have died."

"I told you I was going to Dublin! Aunt Lavy and I went shopping on Grafton Street."

"It's a foolish question . . . but did you buy anything?"

The girl gave her noncommittal shrug, but he checked her with his eyes. She smiled faintly. "I got an Irish knit." Her voice was wistful, almost childish, and she devoured him with her eyes. "A dress," she said.

"Smashing! That must have cost a penny. Poor old Dad! Do we get to see it modeled?"

The girl's face was alight now. For the first time she looked her age. Monica sensed more strongly the feeling the girl had for the man. And more. Something more. It scratched at her consciousness and yet she would not let it through. She was so tired, it was hard to hold it back. It had to do with the man at her side. This sort of thing had not happened for years; she thought she was finished with it. She put her cup down unsteadily on the saucer and rose to her feet.

"Excuse me. I'm very tired. Packing all morning and that hike up the hill." She smiled an apology at each of them in turn. Lyn's face was dreamy and she toyed with a piece of bread on her plate, but her aunt gave an understanding nod. Mr. Hughes's red-brown eyes concealed a gleam of triumph that Monica did not understand. And, because she was so tired and afraid of what she might say, she was overly conscientious in her manners. "I'll see you all at supper . . . Miss Fay, Lyn," she nodded. "Mr. Hughes . . . Doctor Jamieson."

She awoke refreshed but lazy and snuggled down again before getting up. She had no idea what time it was; she had left her watch on the bureau. It was still daylight, but this did not tell her anything; it might be six o'clock. She had just begun to doze again when there was a light tapping on her door.

"It's Mrs. Coghan, dear. I've brought you an extra blanket. It's almost time for supper."

Monica sat up quickly and pulled the covers up to her chin. She had fallen into bed with her slip on and did not like the thought of the older woman's disapproval. "Yes, come in," she said.

Mrs. Coghan came into the room carrying a tray with a folded white wool blanket beneath. Her face broke into a smile at the sight on Monica's stockings on the floor. "You were tired!" she said. "I've brought you a cup of coffee. It'll clear your head.

"Thank you. I can use it." Monica emerged from the covers and threw her legs over the side of the bed. Now that her guilty secret was discovered and not frowned upon, she felt more at ease with Mrs. Coghan. "It was very kind of you."

"Is the table all right? It's the only extra one I had. It's pretty battered and worn. The boys used to build models on it. I got the glue off, but their tools must have slipped."

"It'll be fine," Monica said as she raised the hot coffee to her lips. "I just want to put my typewriter on it. I hope my typing doesn't bother anyone. I'll try not to do it at night."

"This house is pretty noise-proof," Mrs. Coghan said, smoothing the bed. "Mr. Hughes is next door to you and he stays up late anyway. Then he dozes all day long in his chair."

"He's nice," Monica smiled. "Has he been here long?"

The woman grimaced good-naturedly. "Sometimes I think too long. He's an odd old bod. Don't listen to him. I'm not criticizing him, you understand . . . but his imagination does run on."

Monica lifted her suitcase onto the bed and unlocked it. "I like him," she said. "I haven't even unpacked yet. Oh, well, I'll do it later. Did I meet all the guests today?"

"Usually the Fenwicks are here now," Mrs.

Coghan nodded. But they have a grandchild on the way and couldn't come this year. Mr. Jamieson's new here. You won't see much of him, though. Sometimes he isn't even here for meals . . . and he doesn't tell me beforehand. He's a lovely man, though. I think he just forgets. Miss Fay comes every year, poor lady. She's having a bad time with her niece. She takes her somewhere nearly every day to amuse her. I don't think she's very amused, though."

"Who is Mr. Jamieson? I mean, what does he do? It seems strange for a man like that to be here . . . alone."

"I've thought so myself," Mrs. Coghan confided. "And to tell you the truth I don't know anything about him. He's a gentleman on holiday, that's all I know. I could tell by his manners he was all right," she added a little defensively, "I see a lot of people and I'm a good judge of character."

"Of course you are." Monica soothed her. "It isn't our business anyway, is it?"

"That's right," Mrs. Coghan said doubtfully. "If he wanted to talk about himself, he would." She looked at Monica's typewriter and books. "Are you an author?"

Monica smiled as she zipped herself into her skirt. "I'm afraid not. A writer needs problems and I haven't a care in the world. I guess I'm still a student. I came here to do a paper. Are you a Catholic, Mrs. Coghan?"

"Of course," the woman said; it was unthinkable to be anything else. "Are you?"

"No. And it's giving me a bit of trouble, as Mr. Hughes pointed out a while ago. Could you introduce me to the parish priest? I'd like to talk to him."

Mrs. Coghan put a sympathetic hand upon her arm. "You come to mass with me on Sunday," she said. "I'll introduce you to Father MacNeil then."

It was not until they were halfway down the stairs that Monica realized there had been a misunderstanding. Mrs. Coghan thought she wanted to be converted, and she was only doing research on her paper.

Mr. Hughes captured her immediately after dinner and invited her for a walk on the grounds. Only Lyn and her aunt were at the table and they were carrying on a silent dispute. Monica was glad to get away. The day was dissolving into shadow, the flowers strangely brilliant in the waning light of the garden. A gull shrieked against the failing sky. They took the overgrown path to Corrig, and Monica let the quietness of evening wash over her, freeing her mind, as she was frequently unable to do, of every other thought. As they neared the old stone house, she observed that it was even more desolate-looking up close than it was from the Chalet. It had been built to stand forever, but now only the doors were firmly in place and nailed shut, and plywood had been placed over some of the broken windows. They approached it through what must have been a side garden and were confronted at once by the smashed conservatory and a cobbled pavement littered with broken glass. Mr. Hughes paused to light his pipe. "What do you think of it?" he asked.

"It's peaceful," Monica smiled, "but sad. A house broken by the fist of time."

"It hasn't been here long . . . a century or two at most. The breaking was done by the stones of nasty little boys."

"You really don't like them much, do you?"

He sat down on a stone bench with the demolished conservatory behind him. A weary bee, heavy with pollen, settled on his beard and he flicked it away with an oath.

"The plants have grown right out of the windows," Monica observed. "It's like a jungle. I guess nothing likes to be confined. Maybe the boys did the plants a favor with their rocks."

The bowl of the old man's pipe glowed in the semi-darkness.

"I wonder what *Corrig* means?" Monica said.

"A stone house. Very apt, indeed, concise and to the point."

"Then Cor Hill must mean a stone hill. I don't know a word of Gaelic. But of course you do. . . ."

"I spoke Welsh until I was twelve," he said. "Wales is one of the few places where the Celtic language survives. We're bilingual there. We aren't common Gaels, though: we speak Cymric. It has a common root. Gaelic's only spoken in one place now, the Aran Islands. Ireland tried to revive it after the Rebellion; it caught on with a resounding thud. That's why all the street signs are in both English and Irish . . . so people can get around." He paused, as though perhaps his dissertation had been excessive. "As for *cor* . . . it means something quite different. It means twisting, a turning . . . a stirring. I'm not sure how it applies."

"It's *heart* in Latin," Monica mused. "I *do* like this place."

"Miss Rudloe . . . may I call you Monica? I want to ask you something. You'll probably think I'm dotty. Mrs. Coghan does." He paused uncertainly and then said in a rush, "Did you feel anything odd when you came here this afternoon?"

She remained silent for several moments. Then she took a deep breath and smiled. "You must have noticed. I felt very peculiar when I first came into the parlor. I hadn't stopped for lunch. . . ."

"Is that all?"

"Yes. It passed off quickly when I sat down. I remember thinking how peaceful everything was . . . and how you seemed part of it." She laughed with embarrassment. "That sounds silly. It always does when we try to describe our feelings." She paused but he said nothing. "It was probably some trick of memory. I don't remember my grandfather much, but . . ."

"Subliminal levels?" The old man's laugh was a little harsh. "As an American, you must be familiar with the jargon."

"That isn't fair," she said quickly. "Yes, I've studied psychology. But that doesn't mean I see a psychiatrist weekly . . . and none of my friends do, either."

He raised his hand to stop the flow of words and gave a wheezy laugh. "You Americans are too sensitive. You think everyone's against you . . . and it isn't true. But an interesting point came to light in your little tirade. *Why* did you study psychology? It might help me along."

"It interests me. It concerns people, and I like people. That's why I got so involved with literature."

"That follows . . . but it doesn't help much. Are you familiar with the work of Doctor Rhine, Monica?"

She had known it was coming. She had been fencing with him all afternoon. She could almost read what was in his eyes. He knew. But how could he know? She broke the silence at last. "Of course," she said softly. "I don't think he's proven a thing. It's an interesting study, though," she added to maintain the equilibrium of the conversation.

"Have you ever turned cards in a lab?"

"No!" But she was curious to know the direction his remarks were taking, so she added, "Some of us did it once in the dorm. I don't think there's such a thing as the law of averages. How can anyone calculate coincidence?"

"I take it you did rather well on the test."

She took out her cigarettes and he proffered her a light. She had not become used to that yet: it so seldom happened at home. He watched her over the flame.

"It doesn't prove a thing," she said, and he smiled.

"Yet, this afternoon during your giddy spell, you told me two things you couldn't possibly have known. One, that I'm Welsh; you'll observe I have no accent at all. Two, that I'd run away. You were a little alarmed when you said it, as though it popped out unawares. I'm sure it did; I've had it happen, too. Then, my dear, you caused a mild sensation by addressing Tom as *Doctor* Jamieson as you left the dining room. He spilled his tea."

She ran her fingers over her forehead. "I said that? Is he a doctor, Mr. Hughes?"

The old man chuckled. "Apparently. Have you met him in England?"

"I haven't been there yet. I'm going on my way home in the fall." She considered the things he had said. "Look, Mr. Hughes, it may be true. But it hasn't happened for years. I'd come to believe it was just an adolescent sort of thing . . . you know," she said weakly, "like poltergeists."

He chuckled again and sustained it until he broke into a delighted wheeze. "Let me introduce myself. I'm one of the afflicted too. And your famous coincidence has brought us here together, Monica. . . . to a house that's haunted as all hell!"

Later, she unpacked her things without looking at them and pushed them into the bureau drawers. Maybe Mrs. Coghan was right: the old man might be peculiar. But he was very observant, she thought ruefully . . . he picked up her slips of the tongue quickly enough. There was no doubt in her mind that he was "afflicted" as he called it. He would have to be—both afflicted and observant: they went together after all. But this haunted house business was out of the question. She had not believed there were still people who credited such things. She had no belief in them herself. They implied there was something after death, and she had been taught otherwise. Her father was a geologist and an atheist. She had been fed evolutionary theory along with her Pablum. Things were born, they lived, they bred, they died. And that was the end of it. Ontogeny, she smiled to herself, recapitulates phylology. It was the first poetry she ever heard. From cell to fish, to bird, to mammal: birth, love, death, and the end. There was nothing leftover to haunt with, once the brain is dead. If there were, Robbie would have come back to her again.

So-called extrasensory perception was another thing altogether. She did not understand it and no one else did, either. She was sure it was a natural, perhaps even physical, attribute. It was not a gift, as some people maintained, it *was* an affliction.

The old man was right in that. She only had to consider what she had said to Mr. Jamieson this afternoon. A psychic gaff, if there ever was one, an invasion of closely guarded privacy. The man might be anything: she considered the possiblities in medicine. He might be running away from the law. The weight of his guilt would reveal him soon enough. If it was something serious, he would pack and leave tomorrow morning, or even tonight. What on earth had made her say such a thing?

The next step would undoubtedly be a seance, with Mr. Hughes, Miss Fay, Mrs. Coghan, and herself sitting around a table asking stupid questions of the air. She had really stepped out of the frying pan into the fire in looking for a lodging, she decided as she crawled into bed, She could avoid Mr. Hughes, of course; she would be working anyway. But she liked the old man very much. He was human, literate, charming. She could not be unkind to him.

And what was the harm in it anyway? If it did not interfere with her paper, it might be fun. It was like something out of a Gothic novel, or very near it: gloomy Corrig, ghostly footsteps, a seance in the dead of night. Miss Fay would probably get quite a kick out of it. It might even amuse Lyn for an hour or two.

She gave a long sigh as she climbed into bed and burrowed into the pillow. She would have to talk to Mr. Jamieson tomorrow, if he was still here, try to explain her faux pas without too much explanation. The whole thing, all over again.

The room was tilting, stirring: someone was very near. Deep inhalations racked the darkness and they did not come from human lungs. She sensed peril; her heart picked up its beat. It was near . . . getting nearer. She tore herself upward out of sleep with a cry. The room was black. She sat on the edge of her bed trying to dispel the terror of the dream. She shivered and turned on the light to get her robe. It was unbearably cold in the room. Her feet were like ice. Everything in the house was quiet . . . no, there were running footsteps in the hall. She sat tensely, listening, and her heart still pounded in her throat. Perhaps she really did scream out and wake someone; the footsteps might be rushing to her aid. She would look a perfect fool. Cursing Mr. Hughes and his stories in her heart, she thrust her arms into her bathrobe and opened the door.

In the hallway Mr Jamieson was passing in a great hurry, but he paused when her door opened. Miss Fay and Lyn were at their door, too, outlined by the light behind them. Only Mr. Hughes had not emerged from his room.

"I'm sorry," she said softly, "I had a dream . . ."

"It was no dream. It sounded like an explosion," Mr. Jamieson said. "Look, it might be the gas in the kitchen. You ladies better get downstairs in case there's a fire. Knock on Mr. Hughes's door, will you?"

He rushed on down the stairs. Miss Fay tied the cord on her loosely hanging robe and knocked timidly at Mr. Hughes's door. Monica went back into her room for her slippers and wondered what else she should take. People did stupid things in fires; she must keep her head. She decided on her manuscript and snatched it up as she left the room.

"He doesn't answer," Miss Fay said. She had been joined by Lyn in a long woolen, schoolgirlish robe.

"Is the door locked?" Monica asked.

"I didn't try it." Miss Fay turned the knob and pushed the door halfway open. "Mr. Hughes? I say, Mr. Hughes? He isn't here! Why, he hasn't been to bed at all!"

"We better get downstairs," Lyn said uneasily. "Mr. Jamieson said . . ."

"My God!" Monica cried. "He may have fallen asleep by the fire! It's right next to the kitchen wall."

Together they rushed to the stairs. There was no sign of smoke in the parlor. The lights were already on. Outside, a thick mist obscured the night, and running footsteps and muffled voices came through the fog. The light of a flashlight shone dimly against the swirling whiteness and Monica made for the front door.

"Don't go out!" Miss Fay cried with her arms around her niece. "We don't know what it is, Miss Rudloe. Let the men investigate."

But Monica was already on the porch, groping

her way down the steps, the mist wet on her face. She stumbled, regained her balance, and used the plaster wall of the house to guide her with its roughness along the path toward the rear garden. She collided with someone right outside the kitchen window.

"Who's there?" It was Mr. Jamieson's voice. The sound of sirens cut upward from the road below them.

"Monica Rudloe. What is it?"

"God knows. All the turf's been blown clean out of the shed."

"Have you seen Mr. Hughes?"

"He was here when we got here. He and Mrs. Coghan have gone into the kitchen. You better do the same. It's chilly out here." He turned the beam to show her the steps. "Tell them not to light the stove!"

Monica shivered again when she entered the kitchen. It was colder inside the house than without. Mrs. Coghan and Mr. Hughes were sitting at the table with the kettle boiling, and he was fully clothed. "There may be a gas leak," she explained. "The water's hot anyway. Here, let me pour it into the teapot."

"I'll get Miss Fay and Lyn," Mrs. Coghan said, rising heavily. "I'm sure they could use a cup of tea."

Monica avoided looking at Mr. Hughes as she took the cups down, but she knew he was watching her. There was a tension in the room that emitted from his body. He was like a hound restrained from baying.

"You didn't go to bed," she said at last, sitting across from him. "It scared us to death when we couldn't find you."

"I always sit up late," he replied, accepting a cup and saucer. "Thank you. Don't pour it yet! I've nothing against Americans, except that they make a damn weak cup of tea."

"Have you any idea what happened?"

"Haven't you? You've lost something, my dear."

She looked down at her clothes and her hands. "No, I haven't. Oh, God, my paper!"

She nearly knocked Miss Fay and Lyn down as she burst through the swinging door into the dining room. There were heavy footsteps outside the window. The fire department was there, trying to move equipment. She retrieved her paper from the brass coffee table in the parlor and retraced her steps just in time to hear a thick brogue exclaim outside the dining room window: "Jaysus! Watch our for that bloody big stone! I damn near killed myself. How come it's so foggy up here?"

The five of them sat at the kitchen table long after the fire brigade left. Mrs. Coghan had gone to look after her mother while the others drank their tea.

"Who called the fire department?" Monica asked. "It showed presence of mind."

"One of the neighbors apparently," Mr. Jamieson said. "It was the mist. It looked like smoke from the road. The fog never gets up here as a rule."

"It's gone now," Miss Fay said, looking out the window. "Most peculiar. That man said it was the only fog on the point?"

Mr. Jamieson nodded. His face was weary, his graying hair tousled from sleep. Monica felt a pang when she looked at him. He was a remarkably handsome man, and he was really very nice. At least, he had shown himself a man of action when he was needed. And she still had that awful explanation to make in the morning. She shifted her eyes away from him at the thought of it.

"Extraordinary," muttered Mr. Hughes. "I thought it was a sonic boom at first. It shook the windows. And the fog was all around the house. Since there's no pipe in the turf shed, what blew the turf out? You all heard it, didn't you?"

Everyone nodded or murmured assent except Monica, and she confessed, "I was asleep. I had the most awful dream. I though I'd called out and wakened everyone."

Mr. Jamieson smiled. "Is that what you were talking about? You looked frightened to death." He pushed his chair back and rose. "Well, I'm going to bed. It'll take an earthquake to wake me again tonight."

"We might provide that, too," smiled Mr. Hughes.

"We'll go up with you," Miss Fay said quickly. "I'll have to take a pill to get back to sleep myself."

"What kind of pill?" Mr. Jamieson asked, holding the door open for her.

"Phenobarbitol, I think."

He shook his head as he guided Lyn through the swinging door.

"You shouldn't do that," Monica heard him say softly.

She did not like to see him go, and she stared at the door a little wistfully after it had closed.

"You'll see him again tomorrow," Mr. Hughes said and she started. "Very professional, don't you think? The bedside manner and all that."

"Stop it . . . please."

"What do *you* think happened here tonight?"

"I don't know, but I feel awful. It's so *cold* in here."

"We can light the stove now. I'll leave the oven open. Would you like another cup of tea? It's still hot, I think."

"Please."

"Beastly cold, isn't it?" he said with satisfaction as he poured. "Marvelous!"

You're crazy, Monica thought gloomily. You are as batty as all hell. She put her cup to her lips with a shaking hand, and the old man chuckled.

"Are there really bats there?"

Her hand jerked and she poured the hot tea down her sleeve. He grabbed a dishtowel and blotted it up quickly, smiling to himself. "I'm sorry, I shouldn't have said that. Do you still think I'm insane?"

"Does it happen often?" she asked, staring at him with something akin to awe.

He shook his head. "It's worse since I came here," he said. "Before it was just an occasional thing, a flash . . . like you have, I think. There's something about this place, Monica. Don't you feel it yet?"

"I just feel cold," she said. "That oven's not doing a bit of good."

"I hoped it wouldn't. It was an experiment. My dear, haven't you any idea of what happened tonight?"

"No. I told you. Mr. Hughes, what are you trying to say?"

The old man tipped his chair back, put his blue-veined hands over the paunch of his vest, and narrowed his eyes. "I think it was a reception party for you."

CHAPTER TWO

BREAKFAST WAS LATE and the subject of last night's disturbance was avoided at the table. Miss Fay was very quiet and she looked unwell. Her bright blue eyes were faded and a sagging line etched itself from her delicate nostril to the corner of her mouth. She obviously had not taken her sleeping pill. Lyn alone was young enough not to show the strain of a sleepless night. She was carefully made up, her eyes large and bright beneath their mascara, which had not yet smudged, as it had yesterday afternoon. The first thing in the morning, after a disrupted night, she was revealed as a remarkably pretty girl. Mr. Hughes did not come down for breakfast, as Mrs. Coghan said he seldom did. He always sat up late and caught up on his lost sleep in the morning.

Monica was very conscious of Mr. Jamieson beside her, and she ate in silence trying to formulate in her mind what to say to him. It had seemed easier last night, when they were all drawn together by the excitement and sat over tea in their nightclothes. But, now, he had withdrawn again; he seemed very distant indeed. After a curt nod on entering the room, he had not said anything, even to Lyn. He, too, looked weary, but it was not the weariness that comes from lost sleep. It was the fatigue of a mind that is overburdened. It had settled around his mouth and in a deep crease between his eyes, which were squinted against it. Looking at him, Monica felt a mixture of guilt and compassion, which could only be relieved by a full apology.

"I was born in the village," Miss Fay said suddenly, as though she could not bear the silence any longer, and even Monica was relieved when she began to talk. "I lived here until 1922. Papa took us home to England then. The English weren't very popular here for a while. But we came back often on holiday. He didn't sell the house until World War Two."

She was older than Monica thought; no wonder she looked so worn today. If she was old enough to remember the uprising, she must be in her sixties, Monica thought. Sixty and remembering and still coming "home." It was rather pitiful, so she closed her mind against it. Her emotions were too easily reached today.

"Did you live near here?" she asked.

"Right across the road. I'll show the house to you sometime. That's why I come to the Chalet . . . that, and because it's so pleasant here. Mrs. Coghan reminds me of my nurse, Kathleen." She lowered her voice and smiled wearily, as though she knew it sounded absurd. "Only Kathleen was not so practical. She was utterly delightful! She firmly believed in fairies and the pookah and, oh, the stories she used to tell!"

Lyn shuffled in her chair, annoyed by the conversation and Mr. Jamieson's silence and anxious to get away to turn on the portable radio that Monica had already heard upstairs.

Aware of her restlessness and out of consideration for her aunt, Monica tried to make a joke. "Maybe the little people were tossing things around last night," she said over her teacup.

Instead of showing any amusement, Lyn replied in a flat, hard voice, "I've seen fairies . . . lots of them . . . in a mound called London."

The remark did not penetrate the porcelain armor of Miss Fay's innocence: she merely looked bewildered. But Mr. Jamieson's head jerked up suddenly and he regarded the girl steadily for a moment or two.

He folded his napkin carefully and rose from his chair. "Keep out of Chelsea," he said roughly as he left the room.

The girl's face flushed and her eyes followed him like those of a chastised pup. Monica rose to follow him, excusing herself.

He was already out the front door when she reached the parlor, and she went out on the porch and looked around her. It was a clear day, without a touch of the night's mist, and the faint purple hills of Wales were just visible across the Irish Sea. There was a broken stone wall between Mrs. Coghan's garden and Corrig, and the garden seemed larger than it was. She did now know which way Mr. Jamieson had gone and gave up the idea of catching him this morning. She decided to walk to Corrig instead, but she had only taken a few steps when she caught sight of him. He was leaning on a large stone at the side of the house, looking out across the sea. The breeze played with his hair, which was more blond than gray in the sunlight, and he did not hear her approach.

"Mr. Jamieson?" she said quietly. He started and drew up to his full height. When his eyes fell upon her, he did not seem to see her at all. "I really must explain," she said awkwardly. "Mr. Hughes told me I made a gaff yesterday . . ."

He seemed to recall himself to the time and place. "Yes," he said. "Where have I met you?"

She hugged herself with both arms against the chilly breeze and took a deep breath. "I've never seen you before in my life," she said. "I don't know why I said what I did. I know it isn't an adequate explanation, but it's the only one I can give."

He made no comment, but his face showed interest: he was completely with her now. She lit a cigarette for support, and still he remained silent. She felt very helpless, indeed, and looked down at the path.

"It's simple, I guess," he said at last. "You called me Doctor Jamieson because that's who I am. No one here knew it, that's all."

"Your reason for concealing your identity is none of my business," Monica said softly, turning to leave. "I just wanted to tell you it won't happen again. Now that I'm aware of it I'll watch myself more closely . . ."

"Wait a minute," he said, laughing suddenly. "What do you think I am?" When she did not answer he said, "This is wonderful! Miss Rudloe, I'm surprised at you."

He folded his hands on the stone and lowered his face to them, laughing to himself. She did not know what to say, so she studied him carefully. His hands were long and strong and the hair glinted on his fingers like tiny threads of gold in the sun. His hair was cut modishly and almost touched the collar of his jacket.

"I came here for a rest," he said at last. "I didn't mention I was a doctor, because I didn't want to hear any medicine talk. I just wanted to get away from everything." He let his hands fall to his sides, still smiling. "I'm sorry if I've disappointed you."

Her cigarette was almost burning her fingers and she extinguished it carefully.

"You've embarrassed me," she admitted. "I thought you were at least a drunk taking a cure."

"I'm a little drunk on medicine, that's all," he said. "I began to think no one else could cure my patients. I couldn't work a twenty-four-hour day." He frowned slightly. "This slip of the tongue of yours was most peculiar. Do I still have an antiseptic odor?"

"Mr. Hughes can explain it," she said. "He has lots of explanations. He's a frightening old man."

"Evan?" he said incredulously. She reached for

another cigarette and he checked her automatically, with a soft "You smoke too much. Now, what was it Evan said?"

She knew he was right about the smoking, but she lit the cigarette anyway. "He says that he and I are . . . different. You've heard of ESP. . . ."

"Oh, no," he moaned. "I'll tell you right off I don't believe in it at all. My training's scientific."

"Mine, too. My father's a geologist. But things have happened before . . . I can't *not* believe in it, you see. I haven't had anything to do with it: I haven't pursued the subject at all. I've avoided it like the plague. But yesterday it all broke loose again . . . as soon as I came here. I felt so strange . . . the colors were too bright and I was pelted with feelings. It made me almost ill for a moment."

"Has anything like that ever happened before?" he asked with interest, and Monica sensed he was looking at the symptoms medically.

"Not so strongly. The slips of the tongue are fairly common, though. This isn't the first time I've had to make an apology."

"When this thing happens, does anything else accompany it? A headache or a visual disturbance?"

She shook her head. "It's not anything like that. I've never been sick a day in my life. I just got faint. My perception was heightened momentarily. I hadn't eaten," she confessed. He raised his shoulders as though to say "Well, there you have it," but she was not satisfied. "Doctor Jamieson . . . Mr. Jamieson . . ."

"Tom."

"That'll take care of that problem," she smiled. "I don't think you understand what I'm trying to tell you. Believe me, I don't like it at all. And Mr. Hughes upset me a lot last might. I'd like to try to explain. . . ."

"Go ahead, I'm interested. But I can't throw over all my training in a few minutes' time."

"I'm from Arizona. . . .That's in the western United States," she said quickly because she had had to explain it so much during her visit. He smiled and she realized the explanation was superfluous in his case. "My father used to work in mining camps in the summer when he wasn't teaching. My mother and my brother and I went with him as soon as school was out, because we liked to be together. She always hated roughing it, but she hated Dad being away from the family more. My brother was two years older than I and we used to accompany Dad . . . to the mines, the smelters, and rock hounding, just for the fun of it."

"Rock hounding?"

"Rock collecting. When you know something about rocks and minerals, you're a rock hound. Before that, you're just a pebble puppy."

He shook his head, marveling at the twisted tool of language between their two countries. "Go on," he encouraged her.

"Sometimes Dad and Robbie wouldn't take me.

They said the country was too rough. It made me very angry. It bothered me even more, in my teens, when Dad let Robbie go out alone." She paused to collect herself, almost sorry she had begun. The memory was still painful. "One day, Robbie went out with his knapsack. He was sixteen. I was thirteen and had to stay home. We'd been given all the warnings: we'd grown up with them. We knew how to handle ourselves in the desert in most emergencies, like getting lost and running into snakes. Dad even warned us about where we should climb, but sometimes kids don't listen to warnings. I don't know what made Robbie do what he did. He got himself in a place none of us would have thought of looking. One that Dad could not have anticipated. I was the only one who could have helped him."

Her lower lip trembled and she bit it to control it. She did not know what had prompted her to tell all this to a stranger. She had not even thought of it herself for years. Dr. Jamieson did not press her to continue; he waited in silence, leaning back against the mossy rock.

"It was lunchtime," she said in a rush. "Mother had just called me to come in. I was sorting out my collection. I had a piece of galena in my hand . . . I remember, because it was heavy and shiny, and I was particularly proud of it. That's extraneous detail, though, I guess. Then I saw Robbie . . . like a picture on a screen before my eyes." The picture was before her again and she winced. "He was lying at the foot of some rocks and he was crying. There was no feeling connected with it until a few minutes later. Then I felt guilty. As though I'd wished it would happen to him. I know I hadn't, now. I was jealous but I know I didn't wish him harm. I didn't say anything to mother about it. I felt terrible all afternoon. It wasn't until after dinner, when he still hadn't come back, that I told them what I saw . . ."

"You knew the place?"

"Yes, I recognized it at once. We'd been there before. Dad told us not to climb around on those rocks. They were sandstone and half eroded away."

"And your brother?"

"He was dead when they reached him. He died just a short time before. He must have lain there all afternoon."

"Wait. Even if it happened the way you said, there was no way for you to know what the picture meant. And there was obviously a lot of emotional conflict. Otherwise, why the immediate reaction of guilt? Are you really *sure* it happened just like that? Memory plays strange tricks on us. What antecedes affects what precedes in our mind. Don't you see? Your brother's death was a terrible trauma. You probably imagined the . . . clairvoyant flash . . . afterward."

She shook her head stubbornly. "It happened just as I said. It's very vivid in my mind."

He frowned. "You tell a convincing story. I'm particularly impressed by what you call extraneous detail. That's the sort of thing people do remember correctly. But it's something quite alien to my experience. I'll have to give it some thought."

"It was after that the other things started happening. Mother and Dad knew. He didn't like it much, but he accepted it."

"What sort of other things?"

She was on safer ground now. "Nothing very dramatic. I congratulated Dad on his new position at the university before it had been offered to him. And the slips of the tongue . . . those constant, agonizing slips of the tongue! One night, I asked a girl I'd just met at a party when her baby was due, and she dropped her glass. She married a friend of mine two weeks later and their baby was two months premature. They just pop off the top of my head. I have nothing to do with them."

It was the first time she had seen him really smile. He had good teeth and an attractive deep crease cut his cheek.

"I can see how it might not endear you socially."

"It put me on my guard a lot. After a while, it just seemed to go away. It wasn't until I came here that it began to happen again. Do you suppose there's a cure for it? Mr. Hughes has me scared to death."

"I don't think you need a cure," he smiled. "I don't know what to say. As far as I can see you're a well developed, well nourished white female about . . . twenty-two years of age. You may be intuitive . . . I think I can accept that in a woman."

"Twenty-four," she corrected him.

"My apologies. And what exactly does Evan have to say?"

"He thinks I'm responsible for what happened last night. But never mind that now . . . here he comes."

Mr. Hughes walked slowly around the house from the direction of the kitchen. He wore an old cardigan instead of his usual coat and he was staring down at the path. His face was so haggard that Monica wondered if he had been to sleep at all. He did not see them until he was almost upon them, but when he did, his face brightened.

"I see you've found the famous stone," he said. "What do you think of it, my dear? Good morning, Tom."

Tom Jamieson moved away from the stone so they could look at it.

"Have you read the inscription?" Mr. Hughes asked Monica.

"Where? I thought it was just an old boulder."

The old man raised his forefinger and smiled at her. "On one side, yes! But come around here. Tom's seen it before. Tell me what you make of this." He pointed to the side of the stone facing the rear of the house. It was hewn flat and bore chiseled letters on its surface, like a tombstone.

Her shadow fell across it as she read:

*The stone of Joseph of Arimathea
convenient to the Sepulcher.*

She read it again to herself and looked at the men. There was amusement around Tom Jamieson's lips and Mr. Hughes was staring hard at her.

"It doesn't make any sense," she said. "Is there a tomb around here?"

"Not that anyone knows," Tom Jamieson said. "It's a bit of a mystery, isn't it? It has Evan all fired up."

"I can't imagine what it means," she said, studying the stone with interest.

"It means something, all right," Mr. Hughes said. "What do you make of it?"

Monica paused before speaking. She darted a glance at Tom, who made an impatient gesture. "I don't like it much," she said at last. "I don't like mysteries. And I don't like the words 'stone' and 'sepulcher' so close together. They sound ominous. A stone and a sepulcher. The New Testament. I knew I'd heard of Joseph of Arimathea. My religious background's faulty, but isn't he the man who gave his tomb to Christ?"

"Yes," Mr. Hughes conceded without adding any information to assist her.

"I remember, now. After the crucifixion, Joseph gave his tomb for Christ's body to be laid in. And, at the resurrection, an angel rolled the stone away . . . no . . . an angel was sitting on the stone."

Mr. Hughes nodded. "The angel told Mary Magdalene that the Savior had risen."

"It doesn't make any sense at all," she repeated thoughtfully. "Why would anyone put that inscription on a stone in Ireland?"

With his hands in his pockets, looking thoroughly relaxed, Tom smiled. "Don't make the mistake of anticipating common sense from the Irish."

"Tom's right there," Mr. Hughes twinkled. "There may be another stone somewhere in Cork marking the spot where the Gadarene swine emerged from the sea."

"Joseph of Arimathea," she pondered, "that name *means* something to me, and it shouldn't. I saw it someplace fairly recently." She ran her hand over the surface of the inscription and the old man held his breath. She laughed suddenly. "The oddest thing just popped into my head! El Greco."

"What do you mean?" Mr. Hughes asked.

"A painting. A monk kneeling by a cave, all elongated . . . terribly spiritual. I think he had a skull in his hand."

"St. Francis in Meditation probably," Tom said. "They say El Greco was astigmatic, and he used insane patients for models . . . there's your elongation and spirituality."

Monica looked at him with interest; he was a many-sided man. "But what's that to do with Joseph of Arimathea?" she asked.

He shrugged and grinned at her. "Just extraneous detail. How am I to tell you why a woman thinks the way she thinks?"

"I know," she said, brightening. "Tennyson! No, Malory! We used his *Mort d'Arthur* last term as a source of Tennyson's *Idyls of the King*. Joseph of Arimathea had something to do with the Holy Grail."

"Joseph began to wander by the Middle Ages," Mr. Hughes said. "He appeared all over Europe, in one way or another. He's outstanding in the Galahad story."

"The wandering Jew?" Monica asked.

"No, that was another chap. Joseph was a Christian by then. Did you notice anything when you touched the stone?"

"It's granite. It was brought here from someplace else."

Mr. Hughes's eyes were very bright. "What makes you say that?"

"This hill's shale and conglomerate. There isn't any other granite here."

Tom laughed. "That's enough, Evan. Monica's father was a scientist. She has a scientific mind."

The old man raised his shoulders with good humor. "So had Sherlock Holmes," he smiled. "Well, it was a try. I didn't pick up anything, either."

"Pick up anything?" Monica asked. Then she laughed. "Mr. Hughes! You thought I'd get some sort of psychic impression!"

The old man's amusement faded, and he looked a little disgruntled. "It's happened before," he said curtly. "I'm afraid my stone's just a very prosaic one."

"I think I'll go for a walk on the beach," she said suddenly, to change the trend of the conversation. "Anyone want to come?"

Mr. Hughes was still staring with disappointment at the inscription on the stone. "I'm afraid not, my dear. I can get down, but I have the most awful time getting up here again."

She glanced at Tom, but his eyes had taken on their faraway look again. He shook his head slowly. "Another time perhaps."

She tried to work, but her interest was at a low ebb, her subject like dry ashes in her mouth. She rose from the typewriter, lit a cigarette and began to prowl the room, melancholy one moment, exhilarated the next. It was unlike her to feel like that. The mirror on the closet door caught her reflection as she passed.

"Blast," she said, but it was not strong enough. "Damn and blast. What's the matter with me?"

She stopped before the mirror to take a long, impersonal look at herself. A tall, trim girl in dark pants and a sweater looked back at her, and they moved closer together until they stared in each other's eyes. They were blue eyes with a calm serenity about them in spite of the frown between them at the moment.

"You're too tall," she said to the reflection as though it were another person, "and you're getting old. Your cheeks aren't as full as they used to be. They're getting that lean, mature line. You're going to be an old maid schoolteacher, Monica Rudloe."

She flipped her dark hair over her hand and searched the strands in the light. She found a gray hair. In such masses of dark hair, there is always a gray hair or two. She tore it out and studied it with fascination in the sunlight.

"Damn!" she said again and threw herself down on the bed to stare at the ceiling. She thought of all the men she could have married, and the few exciting ones she might have had affairs with. She had never been willing to make such a commitment, though. She was not a cold woman, she told herself. But it always seemed, at the last moment, that they were not really "man" enough for her. Maybe she was too masculine: a tomboy born and bred. It would take an exceptional man to prove himself to her and she had never met him. She had known sweet boys that she was fond of, but who were just like girl friends to her. And the men who might have had her were virile without tenderness. Somewhere in the world there must be a combination of the two.

But what made her think of it this afternoon? Boredom with her paper? It must be that . . . a temporary rejection of academic life. Her subject had gone sterile today and she was making it represent a maiden life. Which was stupid of her, a temporary mood, but she was depressed just the same.

She ignored the light tapping on her door at

first; it did not reach her. Only after it was repeated did she rise on one elbow and say, "Come in!"

The door opened a crack and then a little wider and Lynette stared around the frame. "Are you busy?"

"No," Monica said, sitting up on the bed. "I'm delighted to have company."

The girl looked curiously around her at the piles of books and papers on the floor. The place was a mess, and Monica rose swiftly to empty the candlestick she had been using as an ashtray into the wastebasket. She must ask Mrs. Coghan for an ashtray this afternoon.

"Sit down," she invited, pulling out the chair at the typewriter, and sitting on the edge of the bed herself. "Would you like a cigarette?"

"I'd love one!" the girl said and Monica proffered her pack, tossing the matches with them. "I daren't smoke in front of Aunt Lavy."

"She seems a pleasant enough lady."

"That's just it . . . she's a lady. And ladies don't smoke or swear or do anything natural. It's a bore."

Monica inhaled deeply and relaxed. "I always wanted to be a lady," she said. "It didn't work out very well. When I was seven, I begged to be sent to a boarding school. I don't know where I got the idea; such schools aren't as common at home as they are here. I wanted to take music and dancing, everything. My folks didn't know what to do with me, so they sent me to summer camp."

Lyn puffed cautiously at her cigarette, watching Monica with her beautiful eyes. There was a glint of ironical amusement in their depths. "That's the kind of school I go to," she said. "What did you do at camp?"

Monica put her arms around her knees and propped her chin on them. "Oh, I learned archery and swimming. I was a dead shot with a twenty-two." She smiled without any bitterness and said comically, "I wanted to be Athena and I came out a poor copy of Artemis instead."

"Are you a huntress?" the girl asked dramatically.

Monica did not get her meaning. "Good lord, no! I couldn't kill if my life depended on it. I couldn't even make an insect collection in school."

The girl picked up a paper from the table and glanced over it casually. Monica grew uneasy. She did not like anyone to read what she was writing. Lifted out of context, a page could sound absurd. If affected her like an invasion of personal privacy, but she suffered in silence until Lyn indifferently put down the page.

"You were talking with Mr. Jamieson this morning. I saw you from the dining-room window," she said.

A small shock went through Monica and she was instantly alert. So this was the reason for the visit. She did not know what to say.

"He's a nice sort," Lynette said with apparent unconcern.

"Yes." Monica rose and tucked her sweater into

her waistband. "I guess we talked for quite a while."

The mask of unconcern slipped from the girl's face. "Did he mention me?" Then she tried to cover her eagerness. "I mean, what did you talk about?"

The tortured cocoon of adolescence, Monica thought ruefully; and what a thin-skinned cocoon it is. She was flooded with feelings until they almost made her reel. She was sixteen again . . . and it hurt. She was in love, terribly in love, and it was agony. A blissful, all-consuming agony that she held onto with both hands. She would die of it. Her chest constricted and she could not get her breath.

"What's the matter?" Lyn asked, jumping up from her chair. "You look awful!"

It was the first time the girl had shown concern for someone besides herself. Monica appreciated this and tried to smile, but the realization that the sudden flash of teen-age emotion was actually a transference from Lyn made smiling a genuine effort.

"It's all right," she said, pressing her hand on her diaphragm. "I'm all right, really. I just thought of something, that's all. Lyn, would you be a good girl and tell Mrs. Coghan I'm having lunch out."

She sorted herself out by taking the bus to Dublin. Too much energy was being wasted on things besides her paper. As the green bus turned and swerved through the narrow gray stone streets, she tried to think about her work, but found herself distracted by the events at the Chalet. She wondered if she had done the right thing to move, after all. Her emotions were getting terribly involved with the people at the house.

Finally as they passed through Sandycove where Joyce had lived in the tower with Mulligan, she was able to focus her attention on the author's personality again. She had read a paper by a psychiatrist claiming Joyce was schizophrenic and that he had a schizophrenic daughter to prove it. She could not entirely dismiss the claim that his mental condition had completely deteriorated by the time he wrote *Finnegans Wake* and that the whole book was a schizophrenic play on words; word symbols were something that frequently occured in that mental condition.

The walk to the National Library cleared her mind, and she was ready to work. She walked up the stone stairs to the imposing building with more purpose in her walk. While she was waiting for the male librarian to bring the books she requested, she opened her book of notes and began to go over them on the table. Joyce was a fascinating subject: now, all she had to do was prove in what ways the church made him so.

"Well," a voice said in a loud whisper, "if it isn't Anna Livia Plurabella herself with her hair as dark as the flow of the Liffey. . . . Couldn't stay away from Dublin for even a few days, huh? That country air is bad for people."

Even before she looked up, she knew it was Mirish O'Toole, and she was strangely glad for his presence, though he had lived in the same rooming house as she had in Dublin and his glibness and gregariousness had been one of the reasons she had moved.

"Mirish!" she returned in a whisper, looking up into his narrow face and fine blue eyes. "I should have known I'd run into you here. How is your thesis coming?"

He slid into the seat beside her and said, in even a lower whisper, with forbidden overtones, "Did you know that even Swift was not without vices? I ran into a very tasty bit this morning."

Though the male librarians did not shush them, their looks were enough to freeze the air. Mirish stacked her notes and put them back into the folder.

"I'm finished here," he said, ". . . and you can return later after I've bought you lunch."

She was getting hungry. She did not know whether it was the lure of food or having a sane, if not sensible, talk with Mirish that made her decide. She told the librarian she would be back, to please save the research books, and with Mirish following close behind her and opening the heavy door, she emerged again into the sunlight, lighter in her heart.

"Now," he said aloud in his own musical voice, "tell me all about the sylvan glade you chose over Mrs. Rafferty's. For the life of me, I can't imagine why anyone would desert the cooking odors in that dark hall . . . or the absolutely lovely meals they portend. She had tongue again last night. I swear to God, instead of speaking with the tongues of angels, I'm going to be talking in the tongues of cows!"

"The food's good at the Chalet," Monica said. "It's really a nice place. . . . "

"Well, you don't sound overenthusiastic."

"I was at first. But things have happened. . . ."

"Good Jesus, you're ready to come home to old lady Rafferty's!"

Monica laughed. "No, not that! There are rather a unique bunch of people at the Chalet. I've found myself getting involved. I just want to do my work."

They turned into a fish-and-chips shop and Mirish held her chair for her. "Sure that's what you said at Rafferty's. You moved to get away from the uniqueness of the clientele there. You couldn't stand to hear me telling you that I loved you."

She smiled at him. "You never say anything seriously," she said. "I was safe enough at Rafferty's."

"No one takes a suicide seriously when he talks about it beforehand, either," he said in a mournful tone. Then his eyes sparkled. "Do you want me to say it seriously?"

Monica held up her hand. "No, I'm not ready for that," she said. "Mirish, do many Irish people believe in ghosts? I mean, do you believe in them?"

He looked surprised and ran his hand over his

long dark hair. "Of course I don't believe in them," he said, ". . . not in the daylight. But no one would catch me sleeping in an old house alone at night, either. I feel that ghosts are like God . . . whether you believe in them or not, they're there." Suddenly he looked appalled. "My God, there isn't a ghost at the Chalet, is there?"

"No," she said nervously. "At least, I don't think so. There's an old man there who claims something's wrong . . . and a funny thing happened. No," she protested as he started to give their order, ". . . no chips for me! I'll just have a tomato sandwich, please."

"Hold the chips on mine, too," he said, and when the waitress walked away, "that's one mark Mrs. Rafferty's left on all of us. Never look a chip in the eye again. Now, tell me about your ghost . . . it's still daylight."

"When it's daylight, the whole thing sounds completely absurd," she said and proceeded to tell him about the episode of the turf shed. He was quiet a few moments after she had related her story.

"Anything could have caused it," he said uncertainly, at last. "An accumulation of natural gas from the turf that's stored there . . . you know, like sewer gas. Why is the old man picking on you?"

She did not want to tell him that: she never told her friends. She shrugged her shoulders and took a bite of sandwich. There was a slight pause in the converstaion while she chewed it. There was time to think of something else. She told him about the stone in the garden and, unwittingly, he shivered.

"Look at that," he said, putting out his arm. "Gooseflesh! I don't like the sound of that at all."

"There were supposed to be monks there," Monica explained.

He took a sip of beer. "I like that even less. In most stories of hauntings, there are monks or nuns involved. When I call on you, it will be in the daytime, Monica."

"Are you going to call on me?" she asked, surprised.

"Of course I am! You didn't think I was going to let you get away, did you? I was just giving you time to settle in."

"That's nice of you, Mirish," she said, and meant it. She needed some connections outside of the Chalet to maintain her stability. She needed someone to keep her from thinking of Tom Jamieson too much, to get her away from picking up Lyn's feelings for the man. She felt better already.

"I've just been taking things too seriously, in spite of myself," she laughed. "It really is a lovely little house and the people are very nice. Even Mr. Hughes. I like him very much. Maybe that's why his remarks got to me so much. He's no raving eccentric. He's an intelligent man."

"You don't have to be stupid to believe such things," Mirish said, taking her hand. "Conan Doyle wasn't stupid, and he believed it with all his heart. And I, myself, am certainly not stupid . . . and I halfway believe it, too. Staying at the

Chalet would not be my idea of a lark. My God, you're beautiful. If I were a ghost, I'd fall in love with you. In fact . . ."

"In fact, I must get back to the library, Mirish O'Toole. How's everyone at the boardinghouse?"

"I sense that the subject's been changed. How much could have changed in a few days? Danny's still a revolutionary and Mary Rose still sprinkles bath powder all over the bathroom. I'm a little worried about Danny, you know. . . ."

"Why?"

"He was talking the other night of going North, of joining the IRA. There's trouble enough there without him getting his foolish young head blown off."

"He can't be serious."

"Oh, but he is! Being a bank clerk is a pretty dull job and the blood's full in his veins. What he needs is a woman to think about. Lacking that, he thinks only of the war up there. So, you see, being in love with you is saving me from all that. Being a grad student isn't all that exciting, either. You know, when I get my doctorate, I think I'll shove the whole thing and settle down to write. I'm too creative to be a professor."

"You're liable to create yourself into the gutter." Monica smiled. "But I do think you'd be good at writing. Writers are a little slim in Ireland right now. I wonder why that is? At the time of the troubles, there were too many geniuses to go around. I really must get back to the library and get something done, Mirish. Promise you will call?"

"I will, indeed. I'm a bit curious about the ménage at the Chalet . . . besides being in love with you."

"You're always joshing," she smiled wryly as she rose and gathered up her book of notes. He did not disclaim it, but she knew it was not true. He was in love with her: she felt it strongly. And it would be so much nicer if she could fall in love with him.

When she returned to the Chalet, it was after four o'clock and she was ready for a cup of strong tea. She washed her face and hands and decided to make a raid on the kitchen, wondering if Mrs. Coghan, who was not around, would resent an intrusion into her private part of the house. The maid, Mary, was there alone and fixed her up with a cup of tea and some toast.

"Mrs. Coghan's taking care of the old lady," she explained. "She's not so good today."

Monica sugared her tea heavily in the hope that it would give her some energy. Ever since entering the house again, she had begun to feel drained. "Is her mother ill?" she asked.

Mary was peeling potatoes at the sink. Her shoulders sagged with weariness and her face was waxen. Watching her slow movements, Monica remembered Mrs. Coghan's remark about anemia and studied her closely.

"She's old," the girl said. "There's only one cure

for that, ma'am. And it won't be long before she takes it, I'm thinkin'." She turned on an apathetic tap to wash the potatoes in a collander, and Mrs. Coghan came into the room, red-faced and breathless.

"Get a move on, Mary," she said mildly. "It's getting late. Are they back yet? Miss Rudloe! What are you doing here? Do you feel better?"

"I'm fine, thanks to Mary. I begged a cup of tea. How's your mother?"

Mrs. Coghan shook her head. "Not so good. All the excitement last night. That's probably what's wrong with you, too. Sure none of us had a decent night's sleep. It's bad for her lying there all the time without company. There's nothing to distract her." She washed her hands and began to pound some meat. "She has arthritis. It's painful to move, so she stays in that room all the time."

"How old is she?"

"Eighty-one. It's more years than are allowed most of us, but I wouldn't want it that way."

"I'd like to meet her."

Mrs. Coghan looked up from the meat and Monica caught a faint odor of gin.

"You're a kindhearted young woman," Mrs. Coghan said solemnly. "You're the first person who's ever suggested such a thing." She wiped the flour briskly from her hands. "Come right along with me. Mother'll be delighted, I'm sure."

She led the way into a small hall off the kitchen. It was cooler here than in the rest of the house—a damp, clinging cold from lack of airing, and there were pantries and storage closets on either side of the hall.

"There's a fire in our parlor," Mrs. Coghan said. "It's been a dull, gray afternoon. And after such a lovely morning! I think it's going to rain."

She opened the door to her quarters. The little parlor was pleasant but dark, and the furnishings were not as new as those in the guest house. The couch sagged beneath its chintz cover and there were knicknacks on every surface in the room: china figurines, religious statues, racks of teacups, and several pictures of two smiling little boys.

"Most of them are mother's things," Mrs. Coghan explained. "She brought them with her when she came to live with me. It plays the devil with the cleaning . . . I don't get over it every week." She picked up a newspaper and crumpled it and put it in the fireplace. "Mother's room's right over there. It looks out on the back garden, so she heard the whole thing last night."

The old woman's bedroom was stiflingly warm. A strong fire burned in the grate. Otherwise the room was in shadow from the lace curtains on the window and the angle of the stone wall just outside. When Monica's eyes adjusted to the dimness, she was surprised by the room's austerity. There was a cane chair, a table covered with medicine bottles, the bed, and a crucifix on the wall.

"I've brought a guest, Mother," Mrs. Coghan said brightly, like a nurse on her rounds in a hospital. The tiny figure on the bed stirred and Mrs. Coghan adjusted the pillows so her mother could sit up higher. A small face like a shriveled monkey's peered at Monica from above a thick dark shawl. "This is my mother, Mrs. O'Reilly, Miss Rudloe."

"Light the lamp, " the old woman said in a faint, petulant voice.

The lamp only sharpened the room's plainness, lighting only the corner near the bed. Mrs. O'Reilly was very small, but she looked like a Tartar with bright eyes and thin, crumpled lips. Then Monica realized the brightness was due to excitement: the old woman was glad to have her there.

"Miss Rudloe's the American girl I told you about," Mrs. Coghan said. "She's a writer. She came here yesterday afternoon."

Mrs. O'Reilly motioned her daughter away impatiently. "Go get your supper," she said. "We'll do fine without you. And stop hitting the gin, Peg! You'll wind up like your father."

Mrs. Coghan smiled at Monica as she left the room. Once alone with the domineering little old woman, Monica was at a loss for words, but Mrs. O'Reilly solved that problem.

"My daughter's a good woman," she said, adjusting her shawl with a gnarled hand, "but we see too much of one another. The less we are together, the better we get along. Sometimes I could kill her. She's a nurse, a good nurse. So she treats me like a patient instead of a person. It offends my dignity."

"You're too individualistic to be a good patient," Monica smiled. "I hear you had rather a bad night, Mrs. O'Reilly."

The old woman cackled. "That's what Peg says. She was the one who had a bad night. She was like a bitch wolf this morning." The thin lips twitched into a smile. "Who called the fire brigade?"

"One of the neighbors." Monica studied the old face against the pillows until she realized she, too, was being appraised.

"How old are you?" the old woman asked.

"Almost twenty-five." She did not know why she boosted her age; her birthday was six months away.

Mrs. O'Reilly considered this, her lips twitching in and out over her gums. "Why aren't you married?"

Monica looked down at her hands. "It's difficult to say. I guess the old answer will have to do . . . I haven't found the right man yet."

"Have you tried many?"

"I beg your pardon?"

"How many have you slept with?"

Monica drew her breath in with surprise. Then her eyes began to twinkle. "That's none of your business," she said.

Mrs. O'Reilly laughed, but she moaned when she moved her arms. "That means there haven't been any. If a woman's been loved, she isn't defensive. And it shows on her skin. You're a beautiful girl, but your skin doesn't glow."

"You're an awful old woman."

"I suppose so. There was only one man in my life, God help me. And he was a drunkard and a lot worse besides." She rubbed her wrists to ease their aching. "Did you hear the turf blow out of the shed?"

"I was sleeping."

"It sounded like something tore loose from hell. And you didn't hear it? There was a green flash, like lightning. That's why they called the fire brigade."

"You saw it?"

"I don't sleep much. Oh, yes, I saw it. But it wasn't lightning . . . just before the fog came down. I thought I heard her crying again."

"Mrs. Coghan?"

The old woman shook her head solemnly. "The banshee."

"Do you really believe in such things?" Monica asked.

"As much as I believe in God. Whether you believe in either of them or not, they're there. I'm an O'Reilly. It was my maiden name, too . . . I married a third cousin. We're one of the old families that are mourned."

In spite of the warmness of the room, Monica shuddered a little in the face of such conviction. "You've heard it before?"

"Twice," the old woman said firmly. "I hope I never hear it again. She keened the night my father died, and again the night Jim was killed in that row. Such a sound as you've never heard. Everyone else heard it, too."

"It might have been a cat," Monica ventured. "They can sound terrible at night."

"It wasn't a cat. It was a sound I've never heard anywhere else, before or since. I knew last night, it wasn't her. But it was the same kind of sound for just a second. . . ."

"The fire engines! I heard them, too. It was the sirens, Mrs. O'Reilly."

The old woman gave her a compassionate look and closed her eyes. "I'm not asking you to believe me. I know what I heard."

Monica waited but she did not speak again: she was sleeping peacefully. Monica turned the light off and quietly left the room.

CHAPTER THREE

IF SHE TOLD Mr. Hughes what Mrs. O'Reilly said he might get excited and upset the old lady. On the other hand, it would certainly interest him, Monica thought. He was chatting quietly with Miss Fay while he ate his supper, and he looked harmless enough, but she did not know him very well. After all, she herself was a little excited, not because she gave any credit to Mrs. O'Reilly's story, but because she had met somebody who actually believed in such things.

Everyone seemed a little keyed-up tonight. Miss Fay was very talkative and her color had returned. She had a long nap during the afternoon and was her old self again, vivacious as a hummingbird, fragile as one of Mrs. O'Reilly's figurines. Even Lyn was different. She actually smiled a greeting when Monica entered the room, and she was carrying on her usual flirtatious banter with Mr. Jamieson across the table. She had his complete attention and she was a happy girl. She looked like an Elizabethan player in her gaudy colored stockings, and Monica wondered with admiration how she managed to get so many colors together at the same time and have them look right. She was so pretty, it was a pleasure to look at her.

"I'll take you if you want to go," Mr. Jamieson said. "You'll have to help row, of course. Can you swim?"

"Like a dolphin!" the girl said enthusiastically. "When can we go?"

He looked at Miss Fay. "Tomorrow morning?" he asked.

Miss Fay looked apprehensive. "Lynette, I think perhaps . . ."

"Oh, Aunt Lavy!" the girl groaned. "Mr. Jamieson will look after me."

Miss Fay frowned doubtfully, and Monica saw at once what was on her mind. She was an old-fashioned lady and she did not know Mr. Jamieson very well.

Tom Jamieson regarded her with understanding. "Would anyone else like to go?"

"I'd only slow you down," Mr. Hughes said, folding his napkin. "Besides, small islands annoy me. I'm always afraid they'll sink."

"What island?" Monica asked.

Tom Jamieson turned to her. "Padraig Island, just a mile or so from the coast. There's a Martello tower there . . . and a few wild goats. Would you like to come with us?"

"Oh, would you?" Miss Faye cried, desperate for a chaperone. She did not want to restrict Lyn's activities, but there was such a thing as decorum. "I'd appreciate it so much if you'd go."

Monica was a little uneasy. She felt Lyn would not appreciate her presence on the outing and that Tom had only asked her out of respect for the girl's aunt. To her surprise, the girl said, "Do come! I don't swim as well as I said. If Mr. Jamieson capsizes the boat, you can save me! You know ... Artemis?"

Monica laughed. "Okay. It sounds like fun. But I haven't done anything on my paper...."

"It'll only take a couple of hours," Tom said. "It'll do you good to get away from it." Then he lowered his voice. "How are you feeling?"

Lyn must have announced to the whole lunch table that she was ill. The feelings of the afternoon came back to her, and there was a melting in her diaphragm. Oh, God, she thought, please don't let me pick up Lyn's emotions and be sixteen again. Her eyes met his briefly and she looked away. "I'm fine," she said.

The others had risen from the table, and Mr. Hughes waited until Miss Fay and her niece passed through the door.

"Monica ... Tom," he whispered. "I want to see you. When the others are watching television, slip away, will you?"

A variety show invaded the parlor with its canned laughter: Miss Fay and Mrs. Coghan settled down on the sofa to watch, and Lyn draped one leg over the arm next to her aunt. Tom caught Monica's eye and raised his shoulders and eyebrows, indicating the fireplace. Mr. Hughes was already entrenched there staring at the fire as though it were projected on another screen.

"Evan's ghosthunting again, I think," he said with a crooked smile.

"Ah, here you are!" Mr. Hughes raised his gaze from the hearthstone. "Sit down, I want to show you something."

He pulled a chair closer for Monica, but Tom remained standing as though he did not intend to stay. He leaned against the mantelpiece and looked down at them, half smiling, and Monica realized he was fond of the old man, too.

"Before lunch," Mr. Hughes said, "I sat down here as usual. After all the excitement, Mrs. Coghan forgot to clean. She hadn't even emptied the ashtray," he added with satisfaction. "Look what I found."

He pointed to a spot on the red tile hearthstone at his feet. There was a mark on the tiles and Monica cocked her head to see it clearer. It was not a letter or a picture, just a circular scrawl open on one side.

"What is it?" she asked.

"I've been trying to figure that out all afternoon," the old man said. "I had to put my foot over it so Mrs. Coghan's pookahs wouldn't obliterate it with a dustcloth. It has a feeling, Monica ... it really has a feeling."

She fell on her knees onto the sheepskin fire rug to examine the mark more closely, but she avoided touching it with her fingers.

"I know what it isn't," the old man said. "It isn't a rune and it isn't ogham. It's a . . . mark."

"So it is," Tom Jamieson said softly.

Monica sat back on the edge of her chair. "I don't know much about ogham or runes," she said. "Weren't they Druidic? I've run across them in my reading, I'm sure."

"The runes were Germanic and Anglo-Saxon," Mr. Hughes explained. "They looked something like this."

He picked up a piece of charcoal and sketched a few lines next to the circle: they looked like thorns or chicken feet. "Ogham was something quite different. More scientific and completely impractical," he said. "It was used by the Irish around 400 A.D. to record the Roman alphabet." He drew a long line on the hearthstone and put smaller lines above and below it, in numerical units, some of them slanting. "Each unit represented a letter. I don't know which is which. I'm no expert. But, say, starting here, this was A and this B et cetera. There was no repetition; they had the whole alphabet."

"Ingenious," Tom said, moving forward. "But wouldn't it have been easier to use the Roman alphabet?"

"They apparently decided it was. This was clumsy. They needed the line to begin with and had to write on either side of it. You can imagine a whole sentence written that way. It was finally used only for names on grave inscriptions . . . and it was abandoned completely by 500. By then, thanks to the zeal of the monks, they knew the Roman script."

"Mr. Hughes, you're amazing," Monica said with a smile. "What subject did you teach, anyway?"

"History, my dear. But my interest in the Celts preceded that: I am Welsh, you know. I think my interest in history grew out of my interest in the Celts in the first place."

"What makes you think someone put that mark on the hearth?" Tom asked. "Only a child would do such a thing, and there are no children here. Mrs. Coghan's boys aren't home."

"No," Monica said.

"Then how did it get there?" Mr. Hughes murmured. "I've considered the maids, of course ... a circular motion with a dustcloth that had trapped a piece of charcoal. But the hearth was not cleaned today and the mark was not there when I went last night to check the disturbance. Observe the line, how regular it is."

"It's a perfect circle," Monica said. "That's not easy to make. It might have been drawn with a compass. The broken line at the bottom ... you know how hard it is to close a circle with a compass? You have to sort of twist your wrist around."

"It could have been done with a piece of string," Mr. Hughes considered. "That's the only way charcoal from the fire could have been used. ..."

Tom Jamieson crouched to look at it more

closely, intrigued in spite of himself. An aura of light shone around his head from the fireglow and Monica drew away from him. "You didn't do it, did you, Evan?" he asked at last.

The old man blustered indignantly. "What kind of damn fool do you take me for? Why would I do it? I only showed you because . . ."

"It's all right, Mr. Hughes," Monica placated him. "We know you didn't draw it."

Mr. Hughes smoothed the lapels of his jacket and sat very straight. "What do you make of it, Monica? That's what I wanted to know. . . ."

"You mean does it have a 'feel' . . . like the stone in the garden doesn't have?" She fell silent as Tom rose to his feet. "Yes, it does," she said. The men both looked at her, but it was Tom she addressed: "I'm sorry. I know it sounds silly to you . . . but it does."

"You haven't even touched it," Mr. Hughes said.

"I know . . . and I don't want to. I can feel it from here, and it isn't a nice feeling. Maybe it's just suggestion from talking to Mrs. O'Reilly this afternoon."

"Mrs. Coghan's mother?"

"Yes. She nearly scared the wits out of me. She claims she has heard the banshee twice. She thought she heard it again last night."

Mr. Hughes chuckled to himself and Monica felt relieved. "Her room got to me, I think, back there by the turf shed. It was so dark and shadowy. She said there was a flash of light last night just before the fog came in."

"What kind of light?" asked Mr. Hughes, narrowing his eyes.

"A green one."

"What else?" Tom smiled with exasperation. "The old girl isn't batty, is she? She couldn't have done that to the turf?"

"Oh, no! She's arthritic . . . her hands are quite stiff. She can't move from her bed, Mrs. Coghan says."

"She's probably lying there waiting to hear the banshee for the last time," Mr. Hughes said with understanding. "She probably heard the fire engines."

"That's what I think," Monica agreed.

"Well, it doesn't explain what happened to the turf shed," Tom said and touched his toe to hearthstone. "Or what this is, either. It's put my powers of deduction to work."

"In the Middle Ages," Mr. Hughes smiled, "if a diagnosis couldn't be arrived at, a condition was attributed to the supernatural."

Tom barely suppressed an oath. "We know a lot more now: at least we think we do. We may have made a mess of everything else, but science is still reliable. You work from your angle, and I'll work from mine." He took out his handkerchief. "The first thing to do is clean this off. If it happens again tonight, we'll lie in wait for the culprit next time."

* * *

Screams penetrated the darkness, close upon one another, and Monica leaped out of bed and steadied herself by clutching the bedstead. Her heart beat hard from the sudden awakening and her first thought was of Mrs. O'Reilly's banshee. The room was cold, unnaturally cold—it cut right through her nightgown. Then she realized the screams were those of a woman in panic. She pulled her robe on as she groped her way to the door. There were voices at the bottom of the stairwell: Mrs. Coghan and Mr. Hughes were mounting the stairs. Tom Jamieson emerged suddenly from Miss Fay's room with a set expression on his face. He was wearing only the bottom of his pajamas.

"What is it?" Monica asked.

"Lyn. She's hysterical. I've something in my room. Would you go in to her? Her aunt's worse than useless: she's getting wild, too."

Monica approached the fan of light from the open doorway. The screams had stopped now. The two women were huddled together on the bed. Miss Fay, in a long, batiste nightgown, cradled her niece in her arms. The girl's body was shaking with sobs.

"It's all right now," Monica said, smoothing Lyn's hair back. "You probably had a dream. I did the same thing last night."

Mr. Hughes and Mrs. Coghan appeared at the doorway, looking helpless. They withdrew at once back into the hall.

"I don't know what happened," Miss Fay said,

mopping her eyes with the sleeve of her nightgown. "She woke me with her screaming. She was out in the hall. Oh, it's so cold in here."

Monica reached for the woolen robe on the chair and threw it over both of them. Her head was whirling: she was completely disoriented about time. Had it just appeared that Tom Jamieson had emerged from the bedroom right after she heard the screams? But that was incredible. He must have heard the screams first and got there before anyone else, she thought. Or am I just making excuses because it hurts so much to face the truth?

"Tuck her into bed," he said and she started. She had not heard him re-enter the room. He had put a robe on, but he was still barefoot. "Don't worry. We'll put her to sleep and talk with her tomorrow. Come, Lyn," he said gently, drawing her away from Monica, and the girl collapsed against his chest. She was quiet now, but her eyes were glassy and she was incoherent when she tried to speak. All they could make out was that something had happened in the hallway in the darkness.

"She must have got up to go the bathroom," Miss Fay said. "She must have been half asleep. Mr. Jamieson, are you giving her an *injection*?"

"I'm a doctor. It's just a mild sedative to get her off to sleep."

"She didn't impress me as the hysterical type," Mr. Hughes remarked when they went downstairs later. Mrs. Coghan had gone to light the kettle and the three of them sat huddled beside the fire. Tom stoked up the ashes with the poker.

"Who's to know?" he said. "She might be an impressionable kid and not show it. You haven't been talking to her, have you, Evan?"

"As little as possible. I loathe the child."

"What about Miss Fay? Did you say anything to her?"

"Good lord, no! Her nerves would shatter like crystal if she thought there was anything queer about the house," the old man said. "I've only talked to you and Monica about it."

"You haven't said much to us, come to think of it," Tom said. "Except indirectly. Do you have a cigarette, Monica?"

She fished in the pocket of her robe and came up with a pack, but she had no matches with her. Tom lit a cigarette from the fire and lit one for her with it.

"I didn't think you smoked."

"I'll probably take to drink too, if this keeps up. I see you've been doodling again, Evan." And he pointed to the hearthstone. The circle was there again, in the same place, with the same regular outline.

The old man leaned forward eagerly to look. "I didn't do it! I swear to God I was asleep here when the screaming started. You said this afternoon you didn't think I did it."

"Monica said that . . . I didn't. To tell the truth, I don't know what to make of you. You seemed a nice enough old fellow when I met you: educated and very proper. Now I wonder if you might be a little mad."

Monica was shocked by his harshness, but he motioned for her to keep silent.

Mr. Hughes sighed deeply and looked from one of them to the other helplessly. "I see what you're doing, Tom," he said at last. "Baiting me so I'll get angry and tell you what I think. I haven't said much because people are so suggestible. I mentioned it to you because I thought you might be interested. I told Monica a little because I wanted her to help me. She didn't seem to have any nerves. . . ."

"And last night she woke up dreaming such a bad dream she thought she'd cried out in the night and aroused us all," Tom said, drawing on his cigarette until the ash glowed, illuminating his features. "Are you sure you didn't say the same thing to Lyn?"

"All right," Mr. Hughes said gruffly, "I'll tell you. I didn't say anything to that girl. She would have laughed in my face. She's not like Monica." He looked toward her as he spoke. "Monica's *different*. I knew it the minute I met her. She's like I am. Or like I was. She's still fighting the thing she knows is in her. But . . . she's compassionate. She didn't even laugh at Mrs. O'Reilly's banshee."

Monica laughed now. "It was the first thing I thought of when I heard Lyn a while ago," she said.

"There you have it . . . suggestion. I hardly

mentioned my idea to Mrs. Coghan and she went right to the gin bottle she keeps in her room. She doesn't believe in ghosts, but the idea upset her. I wanted a clear field so I didn't say anything more."

Tom flung his cigarette into the fireplace. "We don't believe in them, either. Is that really what you think, Evan?"

"For want of a better term . . . yes."

"You don't mean clammy ectoplasmic things that go bump in the night, then?" Monica asked.

"Something's been going bump in the night, all right . . . but that's not what I mean. May I explain something about myself first?"

"By all means," Tom said, leaning back in his chair.

"You're a doctor," Mr. Hughes said, "I think that's been pretty well established?" Tom nodded and he went on. "You believe what you can see and hear and feel and smell . . . and what the machines say. That's right and proper: I wouldn't want a witch doctor caring for me. But I wouldn't want a computer doing it, either. Can you imagine anything worse than lying in a hospital at the mercy of a computer that checks your heart rhythm and reads your cardiogram?"

"It's coming," Tom said sleepily. "But what's all this in lieu of?"

"The human element: the thing that's somewhere in between. The physician with feeling, who understands some things he doesn't see. I know you're supposed to maintain a certain detachment. But you can't dismiss everything you don't understand."

"All right, I'm properly settled. You were going to tell us about you."

An abstracted look came into the old man's eyes and he clipped the end of a cigar. "I'll just hit some of the relevant highlights. Otherwise, it would take too long. I'm sixty-seven. Monica's told you about herself."

Monica looked at Tom with displeasure, but the old man chortled, "He didn't tell me. I'm a kind of mindreader, you see. No, not really: I don't know what it is. I sense things about people very strongly . . . I always have. It isn't just putting two and two together, though that comes into it, too. There are some things I just *know*. I knew Tom was a doctor before you let it slip, Monica. You have less control. It's never been that way with me . . . not so subconscious, if you want to use the word. I don't like it myself. I think Freud's division of the mind's processes is all wrong. He allowed for a primitive element, even gave it a name . . . but he did not know there was more to it than that.

"Jung began to investigate it when he was an old man. He did a considerable amount of research on clairvoyance. The results were published posthumously because he didn't want to get laughed off his mountain. That's neither here nor there, except to let you know I've investigated the subject from other angles than my own."

"And you've drawn a conclusion," Tom said. "I can feel it coming."

"Good!" the old man laughed. "There's hope for you yet. Yes, I've come to a conclusion. It's simple, really. There *are* clairvoyants and there *are* telepaths. More of them than we imagine. Most of them don't even know it. Their minds repress it the way Freud's famous Conscious controls the Id. Monica isn't a good example: it's too strong in her. She knows she's holding it back. If she were less intelligent, the result would be interesting. Her control's too tight, though. It's a pity. We should get her drunk or really tired and see what happens. Fatigue works marvels. The lower your conscious resistance, the more it gets through. . . ."

"You make it sound like a seizure," Tom said.

"A brain arrhythmia? Who knows? Maybe we have extra nerve cells that are triggered by known devices. Or we control certain brain waves. Tom, can I will my brain to you?"

"Thanks anyway," Tom smiled. "I don't do postmortems on friends."

"Don't get grisly," Monica shuddered. Then she realized it was no longer cold. "The room's warm now."

"It's gone," said Mr. Hughes. "The room was quite warm before Lyn started screaming. When I woke, a chill had pervaded the house. It was unnaturally cold, didn't you notice? Part of the syndrome. At least, it's supposed to be. It's also supposed to be measurable. I don't believe that, but

I'll have to try it. I suspect the temperature in this room measured the same at its coldest."

Tom smiled and shook his head. "A supernatural nerve gas . . . very complicated, I'm afraid."

"Probably not, if we knew something about it. All answers are simple once they are known. Tom, you're still scoffing. What can I do to wear you down? How can I convince him, Monica? I know you believe me."

"I do and I don't. Some of it I can't discredit. But I don't like this 'ghost' business at all. You're saying there's something outside our minds that's causing the trouble. If that's true, why hasn't it happened in the house before?"

"That's no problem. It's been here all the time. This place is haunted . . . it's been forgotten, that's all. I suspect things have happened here in the past, when the right people were present. I don't know what's haunting it and that does bother me. It's getting stronger all the time."

"Why?"

He patted Monica on the knee and smiled. "I told you. Because you're here now. When I came here, I sensed it at once. But I couldn't get through to find out what it was. That's why I was so delighted to see you yesterday. The two of us together have helped it to get through."

"That's frightening," she said.

"That's enough," Tom said, rising. "Forget it. The tea doesn't seem to be forthcoming. Let's get to bed."

"Mrs. Coghan's with her mother," Mr. Hughes said. "She called her ten minutes ago."

"Very neat, Evan," Tom said. "A brilliant, if simple, deduction, but it doesn't cut ice with me."

The old man shook his head with exasperation. "I'm sorry, Tom. I really am. I need your support and I need Monica. She looks to you for guidance, and I'm going to lose her. It's so important to me." He squared his shoulders, took a deep breath, and looked Tom full in the face. "Who's the young girl who's crying her heart out for you . . . in a prison . . . in the south of England tonight?"

Tom stared at the old man in silence. Something like terror spread from the cornea of his eye outward, until his face blanched. He turned unsteadily and left the room. Monica thought her heart would break. She could not take her eyes off the staircase after he had ascended it.

Mr. Hughes put his head in his hands. "I didn't want to do that," he said.

CHAPTER FOUR

Monica slept through breakfast and came down at ten o'clock: there was no one around. Bright sunlight streamed through the parlor window and struck the bronze coffee table like a gong. Her colors were off again; she was still very tired. The red chintz flowers screamed up at her again from the chairs. She lit a cigarette and it tasted like the first cigarette she had ever had; she looked down at it with distaste. Something was happening to her nerves in this place. She did not like it at all. The sleepless nights were beginning to tell on her . . . or Mr. Hughes's suggestions were taking hold. She discarded the cigarette in the fireplace, and stood looking down at the hearth. The red tiles gleamed dully, with the warmth of their clay coming through; Mrs. Coghan, at least, was up, or the maids had been at work. She passed into the tidy dining room to go into the kitchen, and her attention fell on the stone outside the window.

It *was* strange. Mr. Hughes had been right. Tempered by Tom Jamieson's sanity, she had not felt it at the time. She pressed her face against the glass, squinting her eyes against the sky's hard blueness, and stared at the stone, four feet high and mossy, basking like a green animal in the sun. Its inscription was not visible from this angle; that faced the back of the house.

Why would anyone put such a stone in a garden? Why inscribe it that way? "The stone of Joseph of Arimathea convenient to the Sepulcher." Gethsemane was a garden: it saw the agony of Christ. But Joseph was not there. That was Peter, and he cut off someone's ear. No. The association with the sepulcher . . . the stone of the Resurrection. The stone rolled away by an angel the morning Christ rose from his tomb. With the sunlight warm on her shoulders, she shivered from head to foot.

The door from the kitchen swung open and Monica gave a violent start. It was only Mary, the day girl, thrusting her pale face into the room.

"Would you like some breakfast, ma'am?" Monica shook her head without speaking. "Let me get you a cup of tea. Mrs. Coghan should be back from the hospital soon, and lunch will be on time."

"The hospital?"

"They moved the old lady early this morning. She was took real bad in the night."

"Mrs. O'Reilly? I'm sorry to hear that. Will she be all right?"

"That's in the hands of the Almighty," the girl said with a mournful face.

A sensation of cold settled on Monica's breast. "She's . . . dead?"

"Oh, no, ma'am. But I'm after thinking it won't be long now."

The sunlight seemed to drain from the day. All the colors receded to less than normal, as though a pall had been thrown over the room. Then her shoulders straightened; Tom Jamieson was walking up the path slowly and he was wearing a suit.

"Mary! Would you make some coffee, please? Mr. Jamieson's coming. I'll carry it into the parlor."

"I'd be glad to. And you won't do any carryin' at all. Do you want Nescafé or Irel?"

"Nescafé will be fine." Tom was already inside the door when she entered the parlor.

"There's no escape," he said.

"You've been at the hospital?"

He nodded. "I'd hardly got to sleep when Mrs. Coghan woke me up again."

"How is she?"

"When I left there early this morning, she was clamoring to come home. I'm glad she's not my patient."

"Mary's getting you some coffee. You look tired."

"I could use it," he said heavily and sighed. "Real coffee or that bottled chicory?"

"Something in between." Last night stood awkwardly between them; his eyes were guarded when they looked at her. "How's Lyn?" she asked. "Oh, you couldn't have seen her if you were at the hospital until now."

"I left Mrs. O'Reilly with her own doctor and

came back here," he said. "I've been out to make a phone call. Lyn's fine. She's sleeping. So's her aunt." He laughed suddenly. "What a holiday! It's like an emergency ward. Hysterical females and that cantankerous old woman! I thought she was going to bite my hand."

Mary entered with the coffee tray and put it on the table. They fell silent. She stopped to remove a bowl of wilted chrysanthemums and held them in her hands. "They didn't last two days," she said. "Usually they're so hardy." And she carried them out of the room.

"Sugar?"

"Lots of it, please."

"Lyn will be terribly disappointed," Monica said. "Maybe we can go to the island another day."

"I'd forgotten." He raised his cup to his lips and regarded her over the rim. "You still want to go?"

"Of course. Why not?"

"After Evan's little bombshell, you should avoid me like the plague."

She put her cup down and said seriously, "He was sorry he said it. Don't pay any attention to him."

"I'll ignore him," he said with faint irony, watching her face for so long that she became embarrassed. Her chest tightened until at last she let out an explosive sigh.

"Damn!" she said and his eyes widened with humor. "This whole thing's getting to me. I'm nervous as a cat this morning."

He leaned back in his chair with a smile. "You don't pretend. You're not like some Americans I've known. You're just a Western tomboy . . . and I bet you know better words than that."

She was at ease again; it always helped to curse. "The happiest times in my life were when I was in mining camps."

He laughed. "Let's get out of here. Take a walk . . . anything. Do you want to go out to the island?"

"Not without Lyn. But getting out's the best idea this morning. I'm getting the creeps."

He slapped his hands on his thighs and rose abruptly. "We'll hike to the tower across the road. That should clear our heads. From the top of a hill everything has a different dimension."

The view from the tower extended all the way from Dun Leoghaire harbor to Bray and the air was miraculously clear. The bay spread in a wide blue crescent beneath them, outlined by a narrow patch of pebbled beach. The sky was madonna blue, cloud streaked, tranquil, and the beat of the waves was muted by distance. They sat beneath the stone tower on the hill across from Cor Hill and watched a train below them smoke into a tunnel and emerge again, to be lost immediately in the green trees.

"Twenty-seven gauge," Monica said from where she sat, relaxed and drowsy from their walk.

"I beg your pardon?"

She hugged her knees and smiled. "The train.

It's too small to be real. It's too big for HO. It's twenty-seven gauge."

"I haven't the vaguest idea what you're talking about."

"We used to have a train set. It was very small . . . HO they called it. The bigger ones were on a twenty-seven-gauge track. Didn't you have trains when you were a boy?"

"It was a long time ago," he smiled. "I think it was an animal farm. I haven't had to buy boys' toys since."

He had not been so relaxed before. The lines had smoothed out of his face and there was a dreamy look in his eyes. It was difficult to determine his age. When she had first met him, she placed him in his forties, but now it might be less. A fleeting feeling of sadness seized her. It was painful and she suppressed it at once. Mr. Hughes had been cruel last night, for his own purpose; she would not repeat the incident today. She put a close guard on herself and did not speak again. The silence did not need breaking; she was happy the way she was.

He glanced at his watch. "We'd better get back," he said, giving her his hand. She rose reluctantly and looked up at the tower, which was square and firm and littered with trash inside.

"What was it used for?"

"A lookout, I guess," he said. "You see them all along the coast."

"Who were they looking out for . . . the British?"

He laughed. "The British built them, my dear. You forget we were in Ireland four hundred years. The towers were built during the Napoleonic wars for protection against that little gentleman's ambition. See over there? That's the island: that's a Martello tower there."

"Can we see the house from here?"

They studied the hill below them but all the houses looked the same. She was very conscious of his hand around hers: he seemed to have forgotten it.

"There it is," he pointed, "right down there below us."

Nestled on the top of Cor Hill, the Chalet looked very secure in its trees. It looked different from this angle, smaller, crowded by walls. The whole layout seemed peculiar; she had a difficult time identifying the rooms.

"Let's jump home!" she laughed. "I feel like Lindbergh discovering the Mayan ruins from the air. It looks like there's a wall in the back yard. I've never seen it."

"Yes, you have. It's earth covered with garden. The turf shed's built right into it. I noticed it the other night."

"You're thinking of Lyn," she said. It came out when she relaxed her control for a moment, but he looked only mildly surprised.

"Yes. I want to be there when she wakes."

"You're good with her. You're the only person who's reached her at all."

They started down the path and he helped her

over the rough places along the way. It was unnecessary; she had flat-heeled shoes. But it pleased her strangely to accept his assistance and she clung to his hand.

It was some time before he broke the silence. "She comes from a broken home."

"I suspected that," Monica said. "The whole thing followed a pattern. Her vacationing with her aunt, the way she looks to you . . ."

"Oh, Monica," he said, slowing his steps and finally stopping beneath a tree. "What have we done to them?"

"What do you mean?"

"The kids. They have no values left. They just fill in the silence and try not to think at all."

She smiled and gripped his hand tightly. "It isn't as bad as that. I know, Tom: I teach them. The girls look at some things differently than I do . . . but it's only natural. Things have come fast in the past few years."

"They have no conception of morality."

"You do sound like the older generation," she chided gently. He did not respond to the lightness, so she took another tack. "Values change, too, I guess. You know, when I met Lyn the other day, I made a stupid remark about her name. She looked murder at me; I might have been her aunt. I began to think about it yesterday afternoon. When I was her age, I was three feet off the ground with romantic notions. She's not like that at all. She's *real*. It took me a long time to realize that romance and chivalry are dead. It was a shattering blow. My dream world was destroyed . . . and it should have been . . . it had no basis in reality. Beauty and romance are a wonderful dream . . . but they are a dream, you know."

The gray of his eyes went cold. "What have we offered in their place?"

She looked at him with curiosity. This was a side she had not expected. "Freedom?"

"Freedom is supposed to be happiness. Does that girl look happy to you? There's an emptiness in her she can only fill with loud music and scorn. Do you think she knows freedom from license? She has nothing to hang onto: she's adrift. The world can't seem a nice place to live. All around her adults are analyzing the analyst, criticizing the critic, destroying, tearing down. We don't build anymore: we demolish. We've forgotten how to create. To escape from ourselves, we've picked up our pace, established false values. Then we take tranquilizers and liquor to calm down. Half the country's on tranquilizers right now."

Monica listened with gathering alarm, his mood of desperation communicating itself rapidly to her. "What's happened to you?" she asked softly.

"I don't make apologies. I'm honest." But his shoulders sagged with fatigue and all the anger drained away. "I'm sorry. You're right, I am upset. You can see why I came away on holiday. Everything was beginning to look that way. I can't talk about it now." He laughed roughly. "Even Evan's haunted house is a distraction. I wish to God it *were* haunted. It would provide some relief."

His hand was hurting her fingers, but she did not pull away. His outpouring of bitterness had shaken her and she attempted to gain some control. As sensitive as she was to other people's emotions, her heart felt torn, now, and she tried to cover it.

"Maybe you're causing the disturbances," she said shakily. "You have the strongest personality here."

He laughed disdainfully. "My unconscious is too well trained. It eats out of my hand like a puppy. If it went prowling around at night, it wouldn't be to throw turf out of the shed or go around terrifying little girls."

She attempted to laugh. "What would it do?"

His eyes found hers and held them. "I'd probably break your door down."

The barriers, which had been battered during his tirade, collapsed beneath the intensity of his gray gaze.

He drew in his breath and turned away suddenly, releasing her hand. Staring down at the rocks on the path, he kicked one abstractedly and watched it bounce down the incline to the road. "I'm married, Monica. At least I think I am."

It hurt too much to acknowledge the pain. The hill seemed to move beneath her. She could hardly whisper, "How can you be uncertain . . . about such a thing?"

He did not look at her. He put his hands in his pockets and his face was etched with despair.

"Oh, God," he muttered. "I thought you were telepathic. It would be very helpful right now."

Mr. Hughes's remark came back to her: a girl crying in a prison. It was something she had no right to know. He had not said he loved her; he only *looked* it, and now he was cornered. He was like some fine, gentle animal caught in a snare.

"Don't," she said. "I don't want to know."

And she pushed past him and rushed down the path.

Lyn was by the gate, hardly recognizable without her makeup, and Monica wanted to ignore her, go on to her room. Tears were very near the surface and they would be the only relief. But there was something so touching in the look the girl gave her; it was so full of confusion, she slowed her pace. All the things Tom had said were strong in her mind. She wanted to help the girl if she could.

"How are you?" she asked softly, trying to smile as she approached Lyn. "You gave us quite a turn last night."

Lyn brushed her hair back from her forehead and her eyes were painfully blue. "I'm so *sorry*," she breathed. "Monica, I must talk to you. I think I must be crazy."

Tom was following close behind her. She felt his nearness, so she guided Lyn through the gate and into the grounds of Corrig. "We'll go up to the big house," she said, putting her arm around Lyn. "It's the best place in the world to talk."

The ivy was fresh and green on the broken gray stones of the tower and the balustrades stiff with age in the warmth of the sun. The house reminded Monica briefly of Mrs. O'Reilly. They walked across the tufted stones of the terrace and came to the bench where she had sat with Mr. Hughes on the night of her arrival. The same lazy bees hummed in the flowers, and the bench was cold beneath her skirt. The desolation of the place touched her strangely, and she blinked the tears from her eyes. The girl did not speak after they were seated, she merely stared at her hands in her lap.

"Did you ever see a more desolate spot?" Monica asked anxiously, afraid of the silence, not wanting to think. "It reminds me of Byron. But you don't like poetry, do you?"

Lyn shook her head without looking up. "Monica ... what do you think of me?"

"In what way?"

"Do I seem like a nice girl to you?"

Monica was feeling so desperate herself, she wanted to laugh. She deliberated briefly and decided to tell the truth. "Not very," she said, taking out her cigarettes. Her hand was trembling. "When I met you, I thought you unbearably rude."

The girl shook her head from side to side in the sunlight; there were auburn lights in her swaying hair. "That's not what I mean," she said. "I mean ... a nice girl with men." Her glance darted to Monica's face and stayed there, waiting for an answer.

"Yes, Lyn," Monica said kindly. "I'm sure you are."

Tears came to the girl's eyes and she mopped them away with the back of her hand. "I don't know how to tell you. Last night . . ."

The night before flashed through Monica's mind in three dimensions: the screams, the confusion, Tom so soon on the scene. "Yes?" she asked evenly.

The wide eyes held hers, bewildered, abashed. "I went to Mr. Jamieson's room."

Monica held her hand tightly against her middle. "No! No, Lyn . . ."

"No . . . it isn't what you think! I don't know what happened. I woke up in my room and it was very quiet . . . but I knew something was there. It was a kind of . . . humming. But you couldn't really hear it." She sighed deeply. "I know it sounds insane."

Monica looked at the broken cigarette in her hand. Her mind was reeling. Had she lit it? She searched her clothes for burns. No, she had been just going to light it when Lyn had said . . . She breathed deeply and opened the pack again, took out a cigarette and lit it carefully, holding her right hand with the left, to steady it. As she inhaled the soothing smoke, an impression came with it. Her reserves were low. Perceptions had been reaching her furiously all day long. "Tell me about the noise," she said.

101

"It wasn't really a noise. You couldn't hear it. But it was *something*. It pulled me right out of bed."

"It was a kind of *tension*," Monica said. "A sound in your nerves. Like the humming of these bees only not audible."

Lyn gripped her arm tightly. "You've felt it, too!"

Monica did not answer; she could never explain. "Tell me exactly what happened," she said.

"It was like I was sleepwalking. Only I wasn't. I was wide awake. I couldn't resist. It was crazy. . . ."

"Maybe, but that doesn't mean you're crazy, too."

"It took me to Mr. Jamieson's room." Lyn moaned at the recollection. "I have an awful crush on him, Monica . . . but I wouldn't do anything like that. I don't think he knew I was there until I started screaming."

Monica considered all the things Tom had said earlier. This was what had upset him, released his pent-up depression and brought his feelings to the surface. For a while, up there on the hill, she had had doubts about his mental condition. It had all happened so suddenly: his rage, his tenderness, and her reaction to it. Now, rather surprisingly, the whole thing amused her, especially her own part in the bedevilment of the poor man. After today he probably would not have anything to do with women for a while. "What made you scream?" she asked, returning to Lyn's problem.

"I couldn't stop myself any other way. I don't know what I might have done if I hadn't started screaming. What will I say to him?"

"Do you want me to explain what happened?"

"No . . . I will. But it sounds crazy."

"I'm not laughing. I don't think Tom will, either."

"It will be difficult to explain. It got angry when I started to scream, as though it wanted to kill me. It frightened me so much, I screamed louder. I don't remember much after that." Her gaze fell on the bees and she watched them listlessly. "It was like a whole swarm of them. Like that fellow who was chased by flies. . . ."

"Orestes? It was only one fly, wasn't it?"

"Who's he? No, I mean the one with them all around him."

"Orestes was . . ." But then Monica realized who Lyn was talking about. The suggestion startled her, and her own reaction to it was so atypical that she lowered her voice when she spoke again.

"You mean Beelzebub," she said softly.

"But the stone *faces* the shed," she argued. "It's like a . . . talisman, a charm against evil."

Mr. Hughes twisted his beard in his fingers and shook his head. "No," he said. "Some things I can accept. But the archfiend himself roaming the earth from the regions of darkness? No, my dear. To tell the truth, I don't believe in him."

"I never have either. It was the feeling I had when Lyn mentioned it." She fell silent for a moment; then she added, "They say the devil's greatest weapon is that people don't believe in him."

They had been talking for over an hour after dinner. She recounted Lyn's story to him, and what she had begun to suspect, standing by his chair at the fireplace. Music was blaring from the television set and Miss Fay retired to her room early with a headache. Lyn was sprawled on the floor in front of the screen, barefoot, in a Pakistani shirt and blue jeans. They talked now in low voices so the girl would not hear them.

"What else can it be? I know it sounds wild. I don't think I believe it myself. But what else would do something like that... with all the musical accompaniment?"

Mr. Hughes considered the suggestion, staring into the fire, and he smiled. "What else indeed? We don't know that, do we?"

"The mark was gone from the hearth this morning. The maid must have cleaned it. What does it *mean*, Mr. Hughes?"

"That mark," he said slowly, "is some kind of sign. It's trying to tell us something: I'm sure of it. But we're too stupid to understand."

"It might be a hoof mark," Monica considered, then she laughed. "Our adversary isn't very big if it is!"

Mr. Hughes grinned slyly. "He also looks like a horse. Which is rather reassuring. The devil had cloven hooves, Monica." He studied her fondly. "You've come a long way just since last night. In fact, you've taken a rather startling leap. You were so cold and scientific. Now you've jumped from nothing and hopped right into the arms of satan."

"Well, if you've disqualified satan, who's our next candidate? One of us, perhaps?"

"It's the simplest explanation. But it doesn't feel right somehow." He tapped his toe on the hearthstone. "Even if someone here had let loose a lot of energy . . . the burst from the shed, the sound Lyn heard . . . it wouldn't explain the sign. And no one would try to communicate that way unless he was totally unconscious of his actions . . . maybe a psychopath."

There was a roar of thunder, and rain began to patter against the windows. Lyn stood up with a groan and tried to adjust the image on the television. "It's my favorite group," she cried, "and the picture has gone all funny."

Both Mr. Hughes and Monica laughed.

"It doesn't bother the music at all," the old man said, and the girl shot a disgusted glance from her shoulder. "It's only interference from the storm. It'll be over shortly."

"They'll be over by then!"

Monica lit a cigarette and smiled.

"Youth's resilient," Mr. Hughes said. "Did she talk to Tom yet?"

"He was here only briefly this afternoon. She tried to explain it to him before he took Mrs. Coghan to the hospital. She doesn't think he took it very well. But at least he didn't try to lecture her."

"Is he still upset by what I said?"

"He's upset about something, all right. I wouldn't be surprised if he left."

The old man's foxy eyes became alert. "Not tonight. He's outside the door right now."

She did not have time to react before the door burst open and Tom came in, mopping his face and shaking his jacket, drenched by the sudden rain. He grinned at them. His sudden entrance almost overpowered Monica. She turned away and did not look at him again.

The music died on the television set. Without turning around, she knew that Lyn had silently left the parlor.

"In England I wouldn't have been out without an umbrella," Tom said, approaching them. "I hoped for better things from Eire."

She still could not look up at him. In her peripheral vision, she saw him pull up a chair.

"Well," he said heartily, "what are you witches brewing for tonight?"

Mr. Hughes wheezed and Monica looked at him quickly. He was laughing that peculiar laugh of his, the one he used when he was really delighted.

"Have you jumped into the arms of satan, too?"

"We all have," Tom smiled. "I'm sure of it! I'm prepared to go along with you, Evan . . . up to a point. You won't get me beyond that, though."

"What made you change your mind?"

Tom leaned back in his chair and looked at the ceiling. "Cumulative evidence. It's convinced me, in spite of myself. I also made a phone call this morning." He looked briefly at Monica and back to Mr. Hughes. "What you said last night was true. No one could have known it . . . especially that part about the 'prison.' My daughter always calls her school that."

"Your daughter," Monica marveled softly.

"She's fourteen. And she hates that school. It's a good one, really, but she's always hated it. We'll have to make a change next year, I guess."

"You called her this morning?"

"Yes. She was fine. The call cheered her up a bit. But she had been crying last night, she said. She was lonesome for me."

"What about her mother?" Mr. Hughes asked.

"That's something else." Tom looked back at the ceiling. "I heard the wildest story today, Evan. I don't know what to make of it. Lyn said Monica knew."

"We were just discussing it," Mr. Hughes said. "We think it's true."

"Well, I hope so. Actually, I don't see how she could have made it up. It seemed incredible to me that a young girl like that would . . . it gave me quite a turn. But how? Why? What happened?"

The old man leaned forward intently. "We don't know *how* yet. But that *why* is very interesting." He looked at Monica and stiffened suddenly. "Too many emotions are getting involved in this," he said, sitting back again. "The atmosphere isn't clear anymore."

It was an accusation and one that could not be denied. They fell silent. At last Monica said, "We should clear the air then. It's true. And I know what you're thinking."

The old man motioned her words aside in an attempt to stop them, but Tom said, "Well, I don't! This is the damndest conversation I ever heard. Did you ever sit down to have a cozy chat with a couple of telepaths?"

"No, Mr. Hughes. I won't be quiet," Monica pursued. "We're on the right track now, I know it. You think Lyn did what she did last night because of me. It would have been completely subconscious. . . ."

"That word again!" the old man cried.

"And if I did that, then I did the rest as well. And you just said that if one of us were doing it . . ." Her voice trailed off into silence. "Have you ever heard of the Bell Witch?"

"Who's she?" Mr. Hughes asked.

"It happened to a family in Tennessee in the eighteenth century. A roommate of mine showed me the story. She was gone on witchcraft in our freshman year. It was supposed to be authenticated by eyewitnesses."

"No, Monica!" the old man exclaimed. "Not the devil again!"

"No," she laughed. "Something right in our line. You've heard of poltergeists, Tom?"

"Oh, yes," he smiled. "I'm a Scottish Englishman. My grandmother used to tell me about the noisy spirits. It was always supposed to be caused by a disturbed adolescent in the household, wasn't it?"

"Most often a girl," Mr. Hughes replied. "You don't suppose Lyn . . . ?" But Tom Jamieson laughed aloud, and Mr. Hughes returned to the subject. "No, I guess not. Tell us about your Tennessee witch, Monica."

"There was an adolescent girl in the house. One of the daughters of the Bell family. The poltergeist evolved from her. I guess they didn't know any other word for it. They were country people. But it was a 'noisy spirit' sure enough. It did other tricks as well. Over a long period of time, too. The tales of teleportation were incredible. Everything in the house flew through the air at one time or another. But only when that particular girl was present. And she *was* disturbed . . . obsessed with her father, jealous of her mother. A classic Electra . . ."

"No!" Mr. Hughes cried. "Keep Vienna in Austria tonight. My God, the way that man affected our thinking!"

Tom laughed from the depths of his chair. "You'd be very resistant to therapy, Evan," he said. And then to Monica, "Forgive me. What did this disturbed girl accomplish?"

"The poltergeist finally murdered her father. It got poison into his medicine . . . quite by accident."

"Sometimes females frighten me," he said.

109

Mr. Huges intervened mildly. "I don't think you threw that turf out of the shed, Monica," he said. "That would be quite a feat . . . even for a poltergeist. When I implied you were involved in this, I didn't mean in that way at all. You may be the link, the one who's in communication, that's all. . . ."

"That's where I draw the line," Tom said to him. "There's nothing to communicate *with*. I'd accept a poltergeist first . . . some kind of uncontrolled psychic energy . . . probably sexual. But the ghosts are out!"

Mr. Hughes laughed weakly. "No, Tom, they're *in!*" he said. "Whether we believe in them or not, they're here. And they mean to cause some mischief, too. Let me finish what I was going to say. I want Monica to hear it. And you, too. You may be the one. It's very clear now."

"What kind of mischief?" Monica asked with vague alarm.

"Witness what's happened so far," the old man said. "I arrived here six months ago; it got through to me at once . . . but rather feebly. It fluttered around my head, so to speak, just out of communication. Then you came, Monica. All hell broke loose that night. The explosion, the mist, Mrs. O'Reilly's greenish light, perhaps. The sign appeared, but we were too stupid to read it. It was meant for you. It wanted to communicate with you, my dear, in the only way it could, apparently. Then things began to get muddled. Your emotions confused things. It knew before you did; it was jealous . . ."

"The thing has endearingly human emotions," Tom laughed. "*Jealous?*"

"Yes . . . frustrated, angry. But what could it do? It had no mouth to speak with, no hands to prevent what was happening." The old man was a little breathless and he paused to breathe. "Tom? If you wanted a woman and there was another man in your way, what would you do?"

Tom Jamieson's reaction startled all of them. He rose as though he had been slapped across the face and leaned on the mantel. "That was below the belt, Evan. Watch what you say with that stuff."

But the old man was dumbfounded. "I'm sorry," he said sincerely. "It wasn't like that. It was only an hypothesis."

Turning his face toward Monica, Tom grinned slightly. "I'm almost afraid of him," he said with gentle amusement. Then he looked at Mr. Hughes again. "All right. I'd try to reason with the man maybe. No, that wouldn't do any good. It would seem weak. Besides, I'm a 'ghost' . . . as you said, I've no voice. I could be violent, I guess, but I don't stomach that much. And, again, I have no hands. I don't know. It's easy to say 'fight for her,' but if a woman doesn't want you, what can you do?"

"It wouldn't enter into your head to be devious?"

"I'm not that civilized, I guess."

"Civilized?" Mr. Hughes said with mild surprise. "You're not that primitive, you mean."

"A primitive man would resort to violence," Tom said. "He'd cut the other fellow in half!"

"Not if he stopped to think at all. He'd realize then he'd only lose the woman by such an action. Look at David . . . he sent Uriah to the front of battle and made out with his wife very well."

"A very civilized man," Tom said bitterly, but Mr. Hughes was entirely engrossed in his argument.

"Not all. He was about as civilized as the present nomads in Arabia. And remember the ingenuity of Ulysses? He blinded the Cyclops by wile and escaped by clinging to the belly of a sheep so he could not be detected by the blind giant's hands. To say nothing of the Trojan horse . . ."

"Are you calling the *Greeks* uncivilized?" Monica asked.

"That long ago, yes. They were only a few steps from barbarism. When Troy fell, the Bible was just being conceived in the brain of some Israeli goatherders." He paused to stare at the hearthstone, and leaned forward to pick up a piece of charcoal from the tiles. With a shaking hand, he made a rough, lopsided outline of the sign.

"What's your point?" Tom asked a little impatiently. Then he smiled. "Obviously, you aren't the artist."

"The Celts," Mr. Hughes said dreamily. "My own Celts. Why didn't I see it before? It was a logical association." He looked at Monica. "The sign.

It's on every piece of Celtic craftsmanship . . . a common design. A neck torc, an armband, a brooch! They used it on their tombs. It was to efface the pagan symbol that the priests put a cross into like this." He etched a crude cross in the middle of the charcoal circle, extending the arms beyond it to illustrate. "I think it's the loveliest cross of all. It has a halo around it."

"Evan, you surely don't think . . ."

"But I do. My dear fellow, I really do. For the first time, it *feels* right." He smiled and put his hand to his chest. "It's the only answer!"

"It does explain more than anything else," Monica said. "Mr. Hughes felt it first. It was a murmuring, he said. He speaks Gaelic . . . it might have been trying to talk to him. And there's the stone. It faces the turf shed like a Christian charm. Perhaps the turf shed *is* a tomb."

Mr. Hughes's eyes were glassy with excitement. "Yes. A tumulus, long forgotten, up here on top of the hill." His breath was shallow, his eyes glittered. "Oh, Monica, Monica . . . we've caught ourselves a Celt!"

"Take it easy," Tom cautioned, moving to his side.

The old man indicated his breast pocket and wheezed. "Nitroglycerin . . ."

Tom found the box and Mr. Hughes extracted a small tablet with shaking fingers and put it under his tongue. He closed his eyes and a beatific smile lifted his beard. Monica glanced at Tom with alarm, but he only raised his shoulders, watching the old man carefully. She knelt down beside Mr. Hughes and took his hand.

"You aren't in any condition for these games," Tom said softly. "Now that you know what it is, let's forget all about it."

The old man opened his eyes in alarm. "No!" he cried. "Don't deprive me of this! It's the greatest thing that's ever happened to me. You won't go? Promise me you won't leave. Just for a little while! Until we find out what it's all about . . ."

"I'll stay," Monica said, and she turned to Tom. "What about you?"

"I'll have to, now. Neither of you should be left alone without a keeper. I'm not saying I believe a word of this, you understand. But I'll go along with you anyway."

"Mr. Hughes," Monica said, "what about last night? What about Lyn? That doesn't fit into the picture at all."

He smiled and patted her hand. "It does now. It was that talk about the primitive mind that made me think of them to begin with." He looked up at Tom. "Can you think of a better way to eliminate you from Monica's life than to put another woman in your bed?"

CHAPTER FIVE

~~~~~~~~~~~~~~~~~~~~~~~~~~~~~~

Everyone was better for a night's sleep. The morning meal was pleasant in spite of Mary's untidy serving and, animated by her arrangements to return to England, Miss Fay kept up a steady chatter while the bacon was being passed. Last night storm had blown over, but glistening raindrops still hung on the bushes outside the window, sparkling like fairy lights. Monica avoided looking at the stone, hunched like a drenched Druid at its sentinel post.

Nothing had happened during the night. It was a relief to Monica, but not to Mr. Hughes. He listened and he waited and his gaze fell often on the stone as he spread his toast with marmalade. She wondered what was on his mind, but she was too preoccupied with Tom at her elbow to dwell on the old man. She was not sorry to see Lyn go. If Mr. Hughes's assumptions had any foundation at all, the girl was probably better out of here. A repetition of the other night would make her a nervous wreck. As it was, she had returned to apparent normalcy . . . but with a difference. She seemed more relaxed and childish now, less anxious to enter into the adult world. Her screams in the night might have been the sound of a vacuum breaking, and Monica hoped that it would last.

"Mrs. Coghan will call a taxi," Miss Fay was saying in answer to something Tom had said. "The boat leaves at two. We'll be home by teatime. But you can help us down the hill to the taxi, Mr. Jamieson. We have so many bags."

"I'll do better than that," Tom smiled. "I'll see you ladies off at Dun Leoghaire."

A slow smile illuminated Lyn's face and her aunt twittered her appreciation. Only Mr. Hughes was grave. He folded his napkin with sudden decision and turned to Miss Fay. "You must have lots of memories of the village," he said offhandedly. "You said you lived here as a girl?"

Monica was alert at once and even Tom looked up from his plate.

"Oh, yes," Miss Fay said brightly. "I was born here, and we spent all of our holidays here later. I never did get to show you my old house," she said ruefully, turning to Monica. "It's called Khartoum and it's almost across the road . . ."

Tom choked on his tea. "Khartoum!"

Miss Fay smiled sweetly. "All the names in the village are silly . . . hadn't you noticed? Napoli Bay, for instance. Someone must have been to Italy. And, of course, the Chalet."

"Why on earth did they call their home Khartoum?" Tom laughed.

"The original owner was an officer," she shrugged. "Perhaps he was with Gordon."

"Unlikely," Mr. Hughes said, "but he may have come back with Kitchener. Some of his men came back to build the house, I think. Tell me, what do you remember about the neighborhood? You must have known most of the people who lived around here."

"Yes. There were the Holdens and the Fitzgeralds: I remember them well. And that nice old man up Parnell Road. What was his name?" She sighed deeply. "It was a long time ago. This place was owned by a man named Carlson, though . . . but I never did come up here."

"What about Corrig?" the old man asked. "Who owned that splendid old house?"

Miss Fay's eyes wandered to the window and she squinted them to see the tower of the mansion. "Let's see. There were no children there or I would have played with them. Later, when we came on holiday, a doctor lived there. He had a son. I went to the most marvelous dance in that ballroom! I wore a white dress with a rose ribbon sash. I must have been about your age, Lynette."

"How very like a woman," Mr. Hughes said sardonically, "to remember a dress she wore and forget all about local history."

"Were you here during the uprising, Miss Fay?" Tom asked.

"That was in Dublin," she shrugged, as though the city were leagues away. "The Post Office or something? Papa sent us home when it started. It was spring and the crossing was simply awful."

Both men chuckled and she was mildly indignant. "Well, it was! There was a priest on the boat and I was sick all over his robe." She looked mortified at having brought up such a topic at breakfast. "Forgive me."

"The Fenians were confronting the Black and Tans on O'Connell Street while Miss Fay was being sick on a priest," Tom said. "There's your history, Evan."

The old man wheezed his amusement and Miss Fay said suddenly, "It was a brown robe . . . he was a monk. I remember because I connected him with Corrig."

Silence fell over the table. Mr. Hughes was the first to break it. "Why Corrig? You said a doctor lived there."

"That was when we came on holiday. No, before that, when I was a little girl, another family lived there. Only I didn't see them much for some reason . . ."

"What's that to do with a monk?" Mr. Hughes pursued, his voice steady.

"Corrig used to be a monastery. Didn't you know? It was a Franciscan . . . Augustinian? Oh, dear . . . Trappist monastery?"

"When?"

"A long time ago. Long before my time. Kathleen told me about it . . . my nurse."

"The one with the fairy tales," Tom observed, and suppressed Lyn's mirth with a look.

"Yes," Miss Fay said fondly. "Fairy stories and ghost stories, she lived in an unreal world." She laughed suddenly. "On every mound a fairy, in every house a ghost."

"There are no mounds around here," Mr. Hughes said, "but there are lots of houses. Was there a recalcitrant monk at Corrig, maybe?"

Monica glanced at Tom. He was frowning slightly, making designs with his finger on the tablecloth. Her chest tightened strangely and she looked away again.

"You know, there *was* something!" Miss Fay exclaimed suddenly, and Mr. Hughes leaned forward in his chair. "No. I'm sorry. I just don't remember. It was something . . . bad. I remember Kathleen crossing herself when we passed on the road. Now, isn't that strange?" Her blue eyes took on a faraway look and there were tears just below their surface.

"Try to remember," Mr. Hughes pursued. "Think back. . . ."

"Evan!" Tom's voice was sharp. They all turned to look at him. When he spoke again, he had better control. "This might be painful for Miss Fay."

"Yes," she said softly, her eyes growing moist. "You're right, Doctor Jamieson. I don't think I'll ever come back here again. There's no one here anymore. I've felt it for some time. What the eyes don't see, the heart doesn't remember. I won't be back anymore. . . ."

* * *

Though the sun shone brightly, the path was still wet. Monica's skirt brushed the foliage and drops of moisture fell on her ankles and her feet. She hardly noticed. Tom was at her side talking to Mr. Hughes, his hands thrust deeply into his pockets. They had come out into the garden after breakfast with the intention of investigating the turf shed, but Mrs. Coghan was in the kitchen and they did not want to be seen, so they stood together by the stone, waiting until her chores took her elsewhere.

"Mrs. Coghan was right all along," Mr. Hughes said. "There was a monastery here. I thought it was impossible. The building isn't constructed for it. And now we have Miss Fay's story, too. Local history dies hard, eh? It must explain this." He put his hand on the stone. "The monks must have put it here."

"For no other reason than simple piety," Tom said. "It rather knocks out your sentinel theory."

"Not necessarily. They could have put it here for some other reason. This monastery story really bothers me. I'd like to get to the bottom of it. Corrig just isn't a monastery . . . and never was. It is a very fashionable big house. To me, a monastery means an abbey house and chapel . . . at least a bit of cloister. Corrig has nothing like that."

"A ballroom hardly fits the bill," Tom said. "I shouldn't think it would be too difficult to get information. I don't care much for your wild visitor, but I'm getting interested in village gossip."

"I'm going to the library this afternoon," Monica said quietly. "There's probably something there. I'll look."

It was the first time she had spoken since they came outside. Tom's presence beside her was almost painful, though he seemed happy enough in her company. She was acutely aware that she had made a fool of herself yesterday at the tower. And, because she had never done anything quite like it before, the residue of the experience gnawed at her pride. She did not feel happy at all. The desperate humor of the situation which had struck her when she was talking to Lyn was gone now, and she could not recapture it. She felt humiliated. And his normalcy since only increased her embarrassment. She knew he cared for her; it was too strong a feeling to be denied. But she doubted that he felt anything deeper. He might only be compassionate, as he was with Lyn. The thought of herself as an object for compassion was unpleasant; it made her feel wretched and angry inside.

"How's your paper coming?" he asked easily and she shifted her feet.

"I've run into a wall," she said uneasily. "Only the library can help me. I'll try to get some information on Corrig while I'm there."

"Mrs. Coghan is just entering the dining room," Mr. Hughes announced with authority. "She is now progressing into the parlor."

Monica looked at him in surprise. He savored her amazement for a moment and then laughed aloud as she started toward the rear of the house.

"I saw her through the window," he confessed with a wheezy laugh.

"Evan, do you have bronchitis?" Tom asked, following behind them.

The old man wheezed his mirth. "What's your specialty?"

"Neurology. Why?"

"Stick to it."

They studied the earth wall into which the turf shed was set, a mixture of earth and rock, tufted with grass. The top hinge of the wooden door was broken and Mr. Hughes pointed it out to Monica. "Our famous explosion," he said. "It doesn't look like much, does it? It's difficult to say whether the wall is natural or whether it was put there. You're our geologist, my dear . . . what do you say?"

"I don't know anything about the physiography of Ireland," Monica said. "It didn't even occur to me to look into it. I just assumed that everything in these islands was the result of glaciation."

"Doesn't it tell you anything?"

"The vegetation's been there a long time." She pulled at a clump of grass with difficulty. "It's mostly earth. The rest of the hill is shale. What rock there is in this slope has been there a long time. It's been exposed by erosion." Grasping a sharp piece of stone, she tried to pry it loose with her hand. "That was in there before there were any bulldozers, I bet. Besides, how could anyone get a bulldozer up the hill?"

"There's an artifact known as the shovel," Tom

said mildly. "And gunpowder's been around a long time."

She smiled in spite of herself. "All right. So I have a very modern mind."

"Come inside," Mr. Hughes said. "We have a little surprise for you."

The door fell toward him when he tried to open it, creaking on its single hinge. He propped it open by allowing gravity to claim its lower edge. As Monica passed through the door, she studied the broken hinge carefully. The wood was old and rotten; it would not have taken much to break the hinge out. It was cool and dark inside the shed, even with the door open. She pulled her cardigan around her with a shiver. Mr. Hughes produced a flashlight from his pocket and flicked it on.

"Why, it's a cave!" she cried, looking around her.

"Yes," he said. "The turf shed's nothing but a door on a natural cave. Some ingenious Irishman saved himself some work."

A draft grasped Monica's ankles like hands and she staggered backward until she was stopped by Tom's body behind her. She recoiled forward just as quickly from contact with him. "It's so cold," she said.

"It doesn't get much sunlight," Mr. Hughes agreed. Then: "Yes, I see what you mean."

With the warmth of Tom's presence just behind her, Monica looked around the shed. Stacks of turf and coal were stored along the walls and, at the far end, neatly bundled newspapers and kindling wood caught the flashlight's beam. The walls of the cave were like the one outside: earth and stone.

"I thought you said everything blew out of the shed the other night," she said.

"Tom and Lyn helped Mrs. Coghan clean it up. I went over the walls carefully first, of course. There's nothing but what you see."

"Back home they used places like this to store roots and eggs," she said. She felt distinctly uncomfortable in this place. If Tom had not been standing directly behind her, she would have backed out the door. Instead, she stepped to one side and turned to leave. "That's a funny piece of rock over the doorway."

Stooping his head so it did not touch the ceiling, Tom ran his hand across the lintel. "It feels like it's been hewn," he said. "By hand, too. A stonecutter makes a cleaner edge than this."

Mr. Hughes held his light on the lintel and the gold crown glinted in his mouth. He looked at Tom. "Have you ever seen anything like that before?"

There was an edge of exasperation in Tom's voice when he answered, "You're letting your imagination run away with you."

The old man shrugged, but his eyes were bright with excitement. "Monica, my dear . . . what brand of rock is that?"

"Sandstone?" she said. "Sandstone's mostly red where I come from: this is sort of blue." She reached up to scratch the surface of the stone with her nail. "No . . . it's too hard. I don't know what it is. I've never seen anything like it before."

Tom leaned forward with his hand against the wall and she felt his breath on her hair and tensed. She did not breathe again until he moved away.

"A rather fuzzy expert," Mr. Hughes said cheerfully. "Tom and I know what that rock is, only he won't admit it. I'll give you a pound it's dolorite, rhyolite, and volcanic ash. Sandstone indeed! Tell the lady what the stone is, Tom."

Tom drew in a long breath through his teeth.

"Bluestone," he said reluctantly.

"Never heard of it," Monica said unsteadily. She wanted to move away from him, but there was noplace to go, except through the door, so she stepped into the sunlight. The two men followed and Tom secured the door.

"There are some scattered bits of it in Wiltshire," Mr. Hughes grinned. "Tell her about them, Tom."

"He's talking about Stonehenge," Tom said with amusement.

"Stonehenge! That *is* farfetched, Mr. Hughes."

"Is it? The oldest menhir came from Wales . . . and Wales is right over there." He pointed toward the misty horizon across the gray water. "If they could haul those giants across England, one like this would have fit into their pockets. Except they didn't have pockets."

Monica looked at the purple haze that was Wales, her imagination stirring. "What *did* they wear?" she asked.

"They weren't very dressy," Mr. Hughes smiled. "They went to war neatly uniformed in a neck torc and shield."

"I mean their clothes."

Tom gripped her arm and smiled down at her. "Those were their clothes. If they got cold, they threw something over their shoulders."

A wild sweetness spread from her arm through her body, and she steadied herself on her feet. "Oh, dear," she said and both men laughed.

"They bleached their hair, too," Mr. Hughes volunteered.

"You must be joking."

"No, they washed it with lime. At least they did in Gaul. Caesar described them after he fought Vercingetorix. And the Irish epics mention 'piebald' hair."

She leaned against the stone and brushed its mossy hair with her palm, while gazing at the morning light shining on Tom's hair. His features were in shadow. He was tall and fair against the sunlight. "How tall were they?"

Mr. Hughes's face went dreamy: this was his favorite subject. "There's an armband in the Dublin museum that weighs at least six pounds," he said. "How would you like to carry a couple of those around all day? They must have been giants. From what we know, they were tall, fair, warlike. They revered two things . . . their poets and their women. But even the women were fierce. Their religion, of course, was Druidic . . . something between primitive magic and Merlin. The oak tree was sacred. You still bring mistletoe into your house at Christmas because it was holy to them."

The green moss felt strangely rough under her hand. "They must have been magnificent!"

Mr. Hughes draped his arm over her shoulders and his beard tickled her cheek. "We'll catch one and see."

"Before you set traps, she better hear the rest of the story," Tom smiled.

"Evan's been talking about the Celts . . . who, incidentally, did not build Stonehenge. He neglected to tell you that they decapitated their enemies and carried the trophies home. He also neglected to tell you that there's a good case against them for human sacrifice. Some stones in Ireland have a nasty, ruddy look. They grow moss to cover it."

Monica recoiled from the stone and a smile worked a crease into Tom's cheek. "I just thought I should warn you," he said innocently. "It might not be for love that our friend's roaming the house."

It was an unexpected time for Mirish to call, but, then, he never did anything that was expected. Mrs. Coghan directed him out into the garden where Monica was standing with the two men beside the stone. There was a quick flurry of introductions and Mirish studied them both steadily. Only after they had excused themselves did he stop to look at the stone.

"So, this is the bloody thing, is it? It fairly well

gives me the creeps. Facing the turf shed, too. It's enough to stir one's imagination." But he turned his attention quickly from the stone. "Lady love, I've come to kidnap you for the day. I sold an article and I'm going to buy you the finest lunch you ever had."

"An article? Mirish, how wonderful! I'd love to have lunch with you, but I must go to the library first."

"You and that library. It's fair enough, though. And only the best hotel restaurant in the city will do. We'll have a real splurge, my dear." He glanced at the stone and quickly away from it. "Of course, we'll have to go by bus. My limosine's broken down."

Monica spent an hour in the library while Mirish behaved himself by reading a book of verse. The information she got excited her: she could hardly wait to get back to the Chalet to show Mr. Hughes and Tom. But she tempered her enthusiasm, because she did not want to spoil Mirish's treat, and she did not speak about the Chalet at all.

"Where are we going?" she asked as he hustled her along busy O'Connell Street and past the spot where the statue of Nelson had been before it was bombed by terrorists several years before.

"To the Clarendon, where else?" he grinned. "It's the best hotel in town."

"But isn't it awfully expensive?" she asked, knowing the limited means he lived on. "Maybe we should just . . ."

"Today, we live like royalty," he announced, and there was nothing more for it than to let him direct her in the direction of the fine, old hotel. Her casual clothes were not too casual: a skirt and tweed jacket. And it was obvious that Mirish had dressed for the occasion, wearing a suit she had never seen him in before. However, when they were being seated, she asked for a table in the corner when she saw the smart clothes of the other patrons. Since this suited Mirish's puposes, he did not seem to notice anything peculiar about it at all.

As she held up the menu, he said from behind his, "Now you're to have anything you want at all: filet mignon, salmon mayonnaise . . . Mm. I think I'll have the steak."

Monica ordered the salmon and they were served quickly and efficiently, unlike the other restaurants in Dublin, where the service was slow and untidy.

They were halfway through their meal and Monica was laughing over Mirish's jokes about Mrs. Rafferty's and the people they knew there, when he suddenly went quiet.

"Monica . . . isn't that the fellow I just met out at the Chalet? Or are my eyes deceiving me?"

Monica looked up quickly, just as Tom and a woman sat down at a table some distance away. A shock went through her and her fork stopped midway to her lips. Somehow, it had not occurred to her that there might be someone else in Tom's disoriented life.

The woman was sophisticated and attractive, with pale reddish hair brushed up into a French twist. Every part of her apparel was in obvious good taste and very expensive, and she wore it as though she had known nothing else all of her life. She had style and she would have been quite beautiful except for the set, discontent line of her mouth. Monica suddenly felt gawkish and awkward and young. The woman and Tom were engaged in deep conversation over cocktails while they awaited their lunch.

"Sure you're not going to let that meal go to waste, are you?" Mirish asked, and because it was his great treat Monica gallantly struggled through lunch.

Her first impulse, for some reason, had been to run, as though, somehow, she were spying on Tom. She did not dare glance at them again, but confined her attention to her plate and to Mirish.

"Did you find what you were looking for in the library?" he asked. "You were Xeroxing as though you couldn't do it fast enough. I haven't seen that much enthusiasm over your paper before."

"It was some local history," she said in a strained voice. "Something I promised Mr. Hughes I would look up."

"Still the house?"

"Still the house. It's grown into a psychic investigation."

"And that fellow . . . the Englishman . . . Jamieson, was it? Is he investigating it, too?"

"He doesn't believe in the whole thing. He's only doing it because it amuses him."

"What he's doing right now would amuse me, too," Mirish said, glancing over his coffee cup across the dining room. Monica had her back to the room and did not want to look again over her shoulder. "She's really something. Incredible. He has good taste in women, though she's a bit too smooth for me . . . a little too sullen. Who is she?"

"I haven't the faintest idea," Monica said truthfully.

"Well, bless me, they aren't staying for lunch. They had a couple of drinks, that's all."

"What does it matter?" Monica asked with exasperation, lowering her cup with a trembling hand.

He said thoughtfully, "Sure I didn't think it did . . . but now I'm wondering. What's this man to you, Monica? What do you know about him?"

When she thought about it, she realized she knew very little, and only that when it had been forced out of him. "Hardly anything. He's a physician on holiday, that's all."

Mirish sighed with relief. "I hope it really is all," he said. "I wouldn't want to see you get hurt. From what I've seen today, I think that could happen."

"I'm sorry, Mirish . . . I've ruined our lunch."

But he held up his hand to disclaim any such thing. "Human beings interest me, dear. I like to watch the interplay of emotions. But when it's you . . . I take a deeper interest. We've had a lovely lunch and you haven't ruined it one bit. In fact, you've been a very spunky girl. For a moment there, I thought you'd run out of the door."

"It's very complicated," Monica said. "It doesn't mean a thing. I can't explain to you. A young girl at the guest house has a terrible crush on him and . . ."

But she could not go on. To tell Mirish these things would invite friendly ridicule. How could she tell him, for instance, that because Lyn's emotions were affected, so were her own?

"Why don't you come by the old digs and we can have a talk about more spiritual things?" Mirish said suddenly. "The only way to survive in that place is to be very spiritual . . . that way you don't notice what's around you."

"I have to be home by four," Monica said. "Some of the guests are leaving . . . and I want to say good-bye."

"I'll have you home by then, easily," Mirish said, flashing his white smile, "though, indeed to God, I'd like to keep you forever."

Miss Fay and Lyn were just leaving when she came up the hill. To her surprise, Tom was there, laden with their luggage on the way down to the taxi waiting in the street. Lyn ran down the path to greet her.

"I'm so glad you got here. I thought you'd never come. It's been simply ghastly. Aunt Lavy doesn't understand and she's treating Doctor Jamieson wretchedly. . . ."

"I'm sorry, Lyn. I tried to rush home to say

good-bye, but those green buses rush rather slowly. Why's your aunt so upset?"

"Because I went to his room. He believed me, Monica. When I told him what happened, he said he believed every word. He said nothing would surprise him in this crazy house. What did he mean by that?"

"I can't imagine. Look, Lyn, they're coming. There's something I wanted to say to you . . ."

The girl's face dimmed, as though she were expecting a lecture, but Monica reassured her quickly. "No," she said. "I just wanted to tell you to hang onto your feelings for a while. They're beautiful and rare."

Lyn understood her. Her large blue eyes crinkled at the corners and she smiled wryly. "You are a bloody romantic! I know he's years too old for me. But it is rather nice . . . to feel this way. I wish Aunt Lavy weren't so embarrassed about everything. It's damned uncomfortable."

"Your aunt's a very proper lady. I can imagine how shocked she must be. You must remember that her upbringing was different from mine . . . or yours."

Before Monica could continue, Miss Fay and Tom had caught up with them. Monica avoided his gaze. With a sigh of relief, he dumped the luggage into the boot of the taxi.

"Good-by," Miss Fay said, her steady eyes looking right into Monica's. "You must visit us when you come to England, my dear. Mrs. Coghan has the address."

"I'd like that," Monica said, extending her hand, but Miss Fay embraced her and kissed her cheek instead of shaking hands.

"We really must go now." She glanced at the taxi on the road and her gaze wandered to the blueness of the bay. "I shall miss this place. Well, it's time I grew up."

As Tom helped them into the taxi, he leaned over to say to Monica, "How did you make out?"

Bewildered over her conflicting feelings, over what she had seen today, she could only hold up both thumbs in a numb gesture of success. He gave her a quick grin and disappeared into the taxi, apparently taking the ladies all the way to Dun Leoghaire and the boat. The next moment, they were gone.

Monica climbed the hill slowly, trying to think things out. She loved him, painfully, bitterly, but she would not make a fool of herself again. She did not know how it had happened. She had always believed that things like this should grow gradually, instead of coming in a staggering rush. She was not a sixteen-year-old girl. There was no foundation for a relationship, she hardly knew anything about him. Who was the beautiful titian-haired woman she had seen him with today? She owed it to herself to find out more about him, and about that marriage of his. After the other day, there had been no doubt in her mind about his feelings. What a foolish, impulsive conclusion that had been. She could not remember ever reacting that way before.

It's this place, she said to herself. It makes me feel . . . odd.

She followed the path slowly, as it twisted and turned up the hillside, cutting the houses below from view. Though the day had cleared, the sunlight did not penetrate the slope. It was like being in a dense forest all alone. The foliage was damp and many-shaded green. Everything was still: there was not even a bird's cry. Suddenly she tensed and paused in her climb. She thought she had heard someone whisper. No, it must have been the trees. She looked around her and up into the branches of an old oak tree. There was not even a breeze.

But she could have sworn someone had whispered her name.

Mrs. Coghan served the evening meal to her remaining guests in an abstracted, nervous way. Mary, the maid, was having her sick day, and Mrs. Coghan's mother was home. She wanted to get back to her. The meat was overdone, the potatoes were soggy, and they waited ten minutes for their dessert. None of them seemed to notice. From the time they sat down, between interruptions from the kitchen, they had been discussing the information Monica had unearthed in Dublin, passing Xerox copies from hand to hand.

"It doesn't go very far back," Mr. Hughes said at last. "But, then, it wasn't likely to. Relatively few spots in Ireland have been authenticated and scientifically studied. There must be many tumuli like this one . . . if that's what it is . . . that no one knows anything about. We know who owned these properties back to 1830 now, and that they were once combined. We suspected that in the first place. Only in one place." He shuffled through the papers and held one up in his hand, "is there anything about the monastery legend. It says here the stone was put up in honor of an order of monks who stayed in Corrig for a few years, awaiting completion of their church and quarters. And it says they were Franciscans."

"If you want to pursue it," Tom said, stirring his coffee, "that would be the place to start. It's narrowed down to a particular order, at least. There must be records somewhere."

"Are there any Franciscans in the village?" Monica asked.

Mr. Hughes shook his head. "Either their church never did get built, or it's changed hands in the meantime. We might try a central order in Dublin, though."

"Do you think they'd let us look at their records?" she asked. "Our interest is so . . . secular."

Tom smiled. "That's true . . . and to our advantage, really. None of us are Catholic. But my experience with the clergy here has been very happy. They're good fellows, really, and Irishmen."

Monica leaned back in her chair. "The other day, you and Mr. Hughes were saying frightful things about the Irish. Why the sudden change?"

"It's no change. They are frightful. Look what's

going on up north. But exasperation with them doesn't mean you don't love them."

Monica looked away. So, it was love he felt for the woman with the titian hair. She felt a sudden heavy despondency. Why had she let her emotions get so involved?

Mr. Hughes rustled the papers to gain their attention.

"It says the stone was probably erected in reference to a nearby cave."

"The turf shed." Tom folded his napkin thoughtfully. "And the reference is to a sepulcher. Still, when you stop to think of it, it was a crazy thing to do."

"No crazier than some of the things Victorian people put in their gardens," Monica said.

"Follies?" Tom smiled at her. "There was one at my grandfather's place. When the house was sold, they tore it down."

"The stone's too solid for that," she said. "And dynamite would shatter the windows of the Chalet."

Tom peered out of the window into the darkness. "Well, if they kept it as a conversation piece, they were successful."

"Would you like to get some rest?" Mr. Hughes said suddenly. "I think we should stand watch tonight, together. I think we should sit by the hearth and wait."

"I thought you'd been doing that all along," Monica said. "You never sleep at night."

The old man lit his pipe. "Oh, but I do . . .

that's just the trouble. Every time the sign's appeared, I've been blissfully snoozing, or distracted from my post."

"Last night you slept in your room," Tom reminded him, "and it wasn't there this morning."

"Yes, I may have done something stupid the other night. It may not come back at all."

The swinging door flew open and Mrs. Coghan entered from the kitchen. Her face was flushed with anger. "Would you like something else? More coffee? Sure this hasn't been much of a supper."

"How's your mother?" Tom inquired.

"She's that contentious! She has a very wicked tongue. I wish she'd stayed in the hospital for another day or two."

He smiled his understanding. "I'll look in on her directly," he said. Then, to the others, "I think we're finished."

"Yes, thank you," Monica said to Mrs. Coghan. "Do you need any help?"

"Not at all. You go right in and watch the telly. You're a guest here . . . though, God knows, you'd hardly know it. I'm sorry things have been in such a commotion. Usually, it's so peaceful and quiet. . . ."

"I understand," Monica said, trying to be reassuring. In her heart, she understood too well and felt a little guilty about the whole thing.

"She's been at the gin again," Mr. Hughes said after Mrs. Coghan left.

"I can't say I blame her," Tom smiled. "That

old woman's a perfect harridan. I nearly let her die the other night."

Monica shivered. The room was chilly; it had the feel of the turf shed. She had no desire to go up to her room. There was light and security here, even if the warmth was draining away. "Mr. Hughes?" she said. "What were you saying before Mrs. Coghan came in?"

"Yes, I was about to tell you. The other night, when I was explaining the origin of the Celtic cross to you, I did a rather stupid thing. I drew a cross through the circle on the hearth. It may be coincidence, but the thing hasn't appeared since."

She could not sleep. She tried to turn her mind off, but it played over and over again like a phonograph record. Her thoughts were more with Tom than what was happening in the house. She dutifully lay on her bed until eleven o'clock, and felt only partially refreshed when she went downstairs. All the lights were out in the parlor, and Mr. Hughes was sitting vigil at the fireplace. Apparently it was going to be a dark watch, with only the fire as illumination.

"Can we talk?" she asked in a whisper, and the old man peered up at her, the fire giving his face a strangely satanic look.

"I don't see why not," he said aloud. "We don't know the rules, do we? I dimmed the lights so there wouldn't be any distractions. Tom's with that wretched old woman."

"You're unsympathetic, cruel, and mean," Monica smiled as she arranged the chairs. "Do we hold hands and concentrate?"

"And you're very flip," he said. "Did you have a good rest?"

"Not really. I just lay there staring at the ceiling."

"Are you sure you didn't go to sleep?"

"I will, right here, if you don't stop suggesting it."

There were footsteps in the dining room and a tall figure emerged through the door. "What happened to the lights?" Tom asked.

"It's a seance," Monica informed him.

"Nothing of the sort," Mr. Hughes said brusquely, "it's just more restful without them."

"But we can talk," Monica said. "How's Mrs. O'Reilly?"

Tom stumbled, cursed, and groped his way into a chair. "I've never spent such an hour in my life. I thought Irish women were supposed to be pure-minded."

"Did she find out what she wanted to know?"

His face was mildly surprised in the firelight. "Did she give you that treatment, too?"

For an answer, she laughed.

"What's this?" Mr. Hughes asked.

"The old woman is lively," Tom said. "What time is it?"

"Only eleven thirty. It usually comes after midnight."

"Naturally."

"I don't think you two are going to be much

help tonight," Mr. Hughes said. "You're both too cavalier. Did you know that the Celts divided the time by darkness rather than light?"

"So do we," Tom said.

"No . . . it isn't the same. I'll try to explain. It's a bit complicated. They counted their nights rather than their days, as though they dwelled in darkness, rather than light. The Druids controlled the whole thing. There were four main festivals during the year. It's a pity it isn't November. . . ."

"Why?"

"That was the festival of Semain, when the Dagda united with Morrigan, the queen of demons."

"What on earth was the Dagda?"

"The good god. Don't you see? It was the union of good and evil, darkness and light. Dagda's mate had many names, but he was called the 'good.' She was interchangably Nemain, Panic, and Badh Catha, the Raven of Battle."

"Goodness united with death and panic at what time of the year?" Monica asked slowly.

"November . . . the first of November. On that night, the real world was invaded by the forces of magic. Troops of ghosts issued from the caves and mounds."

"Stop it, Mr. Hughes!" Monica said, rubbing her arms. "I'm not staying up to hear stories like that."

The old man grinned. "It's only July, my dear. But I don't mind telling you that November doesn't sound like a time for tourists."

"Can't we turn on the lights?" Monica asked plaintively.

"I'd rather not. It's the only bait we have."

"What will you do with him when you catch him?" Tom asked. "Is there some kind of circle you can draw to hold him? The British Museum doesn't have one . . . they'd be indebted, I'm sure."

Mr. Hughes's beard revealed a smile.

"Is it just coincidence that your name's Thomas?" he asked.

A clock chimed somewhere and the old man leaned forward to watch the hearthstone. Monica looked at Tom with a covert glance and found him looking back at her. Their eyes met and held in the fireglow; something flowed between them like a living force. Before she could look away, a muffled snarl sounded near them. They all stiffened and looked around them.

"What was it?" Monica enunciated carefully in a low voice, because she did not trust her speech.

Mr. Hughes shook his head.

"Was it you, Evan?" Tom asked. "The way you wheeze . . ."

"It sounded like a cat," the old man said. "No, it wasn't I. Emphysema doesn't make you snarl."

They listened quietly, but it did not come again. They sat at attention with their eyes on the hearthstone. Monica felt she would scream if the silence lasted another minute, but she could not bring herself to speak. The flickering of the fire was almost hypnotizing and she squinted her eyes against it in order to stay awake. Then the coldness descended, not by degrees, but all at once like a blast from a tomb. Mr. Hughes reached out to grasp her hand.

"My God," Tom said, and then he drew in his breath with a cry and pushed his head against the back of the chair, clawing at his throat with his hands. His face was white and he was struggling for breath. Monica rose from her chair with alarm.

"He's choking," she cried. "Do something! He can't breathe."

From the depths of his struggle, Tom waved her aside, shaking his head widely. As quickly as the attack came on, it subsided, leaving him pale and shaken in his chair. He sighed out a curse and rubbed his throat without speaking. He was still breathing heavily. Mr. Hughes turned on the light and they both bent over him.

"What is it? Are you all right?"

Tom shook his head slowly from side to side and drew in a deep breath. He exhaled it slowly, rubbing his throat. "I couldn't breathe. My throat constricted. It was like being strangled. . . ."

"Has it ever happened before?"

"No." He loosened his tie and pulled it off. They were all silent for a moment, then he said, "Hysteria. It's the only thing it could have been. But I've never had an hysterical symptom in my life."

"Maybe you were more tense than you thought you were," Monica suggested. She was grateful that it was over, but her hands were still trembling.

"Are you sure that's all it was?" Mr. Hughes asked, regaining his chair. He, too, was shaken. All the color had left his face.

Tom nodded thoughtfully. "It's the only thing it could have been. Laryngospasm. As though pressure was being put on my neck from outside. Do you suppose it could have been that liquid chicory Mrs. Coghan serves as coffee? The panic reaction was like anaphalactic shock." His smile was a little desperate. "But I'm not allergic, either."

Monica sat back on her heels and looked at him. He reached out suddenly and took her hand. "Thanks for not attempting first aid. You might have killed me."

"I wouldn't have known what to do. I was so frightened."

"You're hand's like ice," he said, studying her.

"It's back again," Mr. Hughes said suddenly. "You diverted our attention. It's added something, too."

The sign was on the hearthstone, big and bold and black, as though it had been scrawled in anger. But it was not an open circle anymore. One of the ends had been carried upward into a spiral whirl, concluding in another open end in the middle.

"It's stronger tonight," Mr. Hughes said, tracing the pattern with his pipestem. "It *is* a Celtic design."

"Like a whirlpool," Monica said, "twisting, turning . . ."

"*Cor!*" Mr. Hughes exclaimed. "The name of the hill."

"What is it trying to say?"

There was a knock on Monica's door just as she was getting into bed. She picked up her robe and struggled into it.

"Who is it?" she asked fearfully.

"Tom. I want to talk to you."

She opened the door a crack and looked out from her lighted room. "Are you all right?"

"Yes . . . yes, I'm fine. Are you all right, Monica?"

"Aside from being scared out of my wits, yes," she said.

"May I come in for a moment? I'd really like to talk to you."

She hestitated a moment; then, "No, I don't think so . . . it's late. What do you want to say?"

"I can't talk through the door. Will you come out here?"

She opened the door and slipped out into the cold hall, the light from the room illuminating a section, so that she could see his face.

"You've been . . . different tonight. Is something wrong?" he asked and she shifted her gaze. "Monica, what is this Mirish fellow to you?"

She was shocked by the words. As though he had any reason to know about Mirish, when he kept his own assignations to himself. Should she

145

respond with a similar question? No, she was too proud, she could not stoop to it.

"I'm very fond of him," she said steadily, trying to avoid his eyes.

"And he's in love with you," Tom replied.

"He thinks he is," she said. This was really too much; she did not know how to handle it. She wanted to flee into her room and shut the door in his face. She felt nervous, without any reason for feeling so; ordinarily, she could have answered such questions without the words sticking in her throat. What was this man, anyway? She did not know him at all. He might be the greatest womanizer in England for all that she knew. She was not going to be anyone's toy.

"It's really late," she said. "I'm exhausted . . ."

"Sorry . . . I didn't mean to be a bore." His voice had taken on a formality which she had not observed in him before. "I'll say goodnight, then."

"Yes . . . goodnight," she said, putting the door once again between them and closing it quietly. She heard his steps retreat down the hall and leaned her back miserably against the closed door. Now she had really done the wrong thing . . . or had she? He was a married man . . . . and he had another woman in Dublin, a beautiful, sophisticated woman, who was more his sort. Why was he trying to force his attentions on Monica? She had never been involved with a married man before, and it was better that she cut if off quickly, before she became further entangled and hurt. She did not want a love affair with Tom: her feelings went deeper than that. There were too many women in his life already. It was better to stay on the sidelines while she was here at the Chalet. That way, he would never be an experience of which she would be ashamed. Accept her feelings for him for what they probably were . . . a crush like Lyn's.

But when she pulled her robe off and curled up between the cold sheets, she knew that all of her admonitions to herself were not enough. Perhaps she should pack and leave immediately, put him behind her once and for all. She could not do that, though: she had promised Mr. Hughes.

When it came right down to it, the manifestations in the house were all any of them should be concentrating on. Monica was only too convinced, that there *was* something here, after the episode this evening. She would put all her attention on that and forget about red-headed women and wives. Forget about Tom, as a man, if she could.

Overcome by exhaustion, her consciousness was snuffed like a light. She dreamed she was at home, riding across the desert on a little pinto mare. Her hair was blowing and she felt young and joyously free. But, then, a cloud went over the sun, a gray storm passed overhead and she realized that her horse's hoofbeats were not the only ones in the solitary place. They were accompanied by others which beat hard and fierce in pursuit of her. She had a sinking feeling, a sensation of pure horror as looking back over her shoulder, she saw a powerful black stallion, unmounted, in wild pursuit.

She lit a cigarette and leaned her chair back to stare out the window of her room. The men had gone to Dublin, and the house was quiet without them. She could not even hear Mrs. Coghan moving around downstairs. The green treetops outside her window moved languidly in the breeze from the water and she was struck once again with the beauty of the point when the sun was shining.

The residue of last night's experience lay heavy upon Tom this morning. He looked tired and drawn. Neither he nor Mr. Hughes wanted to leave her alone while they went to the monastery, but she wanted to stay. She needed some time alone. Tom tried to laugh off what had happened by the fire by saying he hoped Mr. Hughes was right. It would be far nicer to be attacked by a "real phantom" than disturbed in one's nerves.

He winked at her when they left. "We're off to track down your demon lover," he said. "I'm not sure I like him. Don't go wandering about the grounds today, please. I haven't come around to Evan's way of thinking all the way, but I wish you'd stay in your room."

And she had been in her room for several hours, doing a little desultory research for her paper, smoking too many cigarettes, and trying not to think about last night. She could not get the thought out of her mind that, whatever happened, she had been the cause. It was the same way she had felt after Robbie's death. She was an unknown quantity, even to herself. Though she had never made a conscious death wish in her life, she felt burdened with guilt when someone she loved was hurt. Was it possible that her clairvoyant sickness was the disturbance itself? She might be sick, really sick, and not know it. But a psychotic is not supposed to question his own sanity, as she was questioning hers. On the other hand, with her perception, perhaps insanity had taken another turn. She had been trying to resist loving Tom because he was married. This resistance was conscious. But what was happening in her unconscious in the process? Was she guarding herself so fiercely that she had attacked him? To protect herself, had she tried to strangle him to death?

Her cigarette burnt her fingers and she jumped up to put it out. The thought was too fantastic. In her heart, she knew she was not like that. And if she had not done it, someone else had. She had come to the moment of truth, and she knew it. The moment of acceptance. After all her scientific and psychological arguments had failed, she must now, for the first time in her life, accept something else, and she knew that acceptance was commitment.

She walked to the window and sat down on the sill. The hilltop seemed incredibly ancient with its gray stones and green foliage and its eternal view of the water. Her mind began to drift backward into time . . . and there were no houses on the point. Corrig's tower was erased from the sky. The place was so quiet, so peaceful. She relaxed the tight hold on her mind and let it drift. Below her, the hill shifted subtly, darkened, and mist began to creep between the branches of the trees. All sound was suspended, as though she had suddenly gone deaf, but she felt no alarm. A fire blazed suddenly, like an orange flower in the gray-green mist, where Corrig should have been. Images began to cross her mind swiftly, like film drawn too fast through a projector, and she let them come. A procession wound its way slowly up the hill beside a wall, the horses in green-bronze trappings stepped gingerly through the swelling fog on the ground. Her perception moved in closer, trying to discern the faces of the gray riders, but they were too misty. Only their green-gold hair was visible, and the spiral design on their shoulder brooches. They dismounted and drank from large bronze basins arranged in a circle around the fire, and she realized it was a festival and that she must go out to join them. Three loud knocks in the room made her blind her eyes.

"Miss Rudloe! I hope you aren't resting."

Her senses drew in like scorched petals; her heart beat uncomfortably. The treetops below waved bright green in the sunlight and a raven cried out as it flew from a pine. She touched her face with her hand. "No," she said with a feeling of unreality. "What is it, Mrs. Coghan?"

"We have a visitor. Father MacNeil's here."

She did not want to open the door. She felt exhausted and wanted to sort this thing out. But habit was too strong; she could not be impolite.

Steeling herself for an unpleasant encounter, she finally went to the door.

The priest had a round red face and his hair was thin on top. He smelled faintly of incense and whisky, subtly combined, and he gave her a congenial smile.

"Sorry to bother you. Are you enjoying your stay?"

Monica nodded uncertainly; her hands were shaking. She tried to think of something to say. The priest and Mrs. Coghan stood in the hallway looking at her, and she wondered if she appeared as peculiar as she felt. "Mrs. Coghan didn't tell me you were coming," she brought out at last.

He threw his hands up and made a comical face. "All of a sudden, she wants the house blessed! Not tomorrow or next week . . . but right now. So here I am," he shrugged.

"I'll get the crucifix, Father," Mrs. Coghan said; and then, to Monica, "It won't take long. I'm sorry to disturb you."

When she disappeared down the stairs, Monica did not know whether to invite the priest into her room or not. She stood awkwardly at the door and attempted to smile. "The house *blessed*?" she asked.

Thoughts of exorcism crossed her mind. She wished Mr. Hughes and Tom were her. But the priest reassured her.

"It's a pleasant little ritual. I sprinkle holy water and say a few prayers. Then the house is safe for a while."

"Safe from what?"

His eyes twinkled. "Bad things. The poor woman's worried about her mother, I think. It would reassure her to have it done."

"It isn't an exorcism, then?"

A laugh exploded from his ruddy face. "Good heavens, no! We don't cater to superstition. Do you have a little devil tucked up your sleeve somewhere?"

"I don't know," she said numbly, then she attempted to smile. "You mean there isn't an exorcism rite anymore?"

"Oh, there's probaly one knocking about the books somewhere. I don't know it. No one else does either, I suspect. It just isn't used."

Mrs. Coghan returned, out of breath from climbing the stairs, carrying a large crucifix.

"This thing's too heavy to carry around," she complained good-naturedly. "I used to have a nursing home," she said to Monica. "I kept this for the last rites."

The priest smiled. "The strength of your faith should make it light as a feather."

Monica did not want to intrude on their ceremony, though it would have interested her at any other time. She just wanted to get away. "I'll go down and see your mother," she said to Mrs. Coghan. "Can I make a pot of tea?"

"Of coure. There's water in the electric kettle; just plug it in. She wasn't very happy when we left her. I hope she isn't rude to you."

* * *

As she passed the dining-room window, she looked at the stone and over its head to Corrig. The tower was standing solid and ivied against the blue sky, as though it had been there forever. What had happened a few minutes ago in her room was too overpowering; she decided not to think of it right now. She felt weak and shaky and needed a good, strong cup of tea.

The copper kettle was all prepared, as Mrs. Coghan had said, but she had a little trouble finding the electric outlet. She had not been in the kitchen before to prepare any food. Once she got the kettle going, she set about opening all the cupboards to find cups and silverware and a tray. The kitchen was clean and well organized and she soon had everything together. At least she knew where the tea was; she had seen Mary take it out several times. But when she found it, she was faced with the problem of what to do with it. The only tea she had ever made was with a teabag, and her mother had not even had that at home. The Rudloes were coffee drinkers. She decided to put the tea in the pot first and pour hot water over it, the way she made instant coffee, and hope that it would work. She remembered Mr. Hughes's warning about having the water on the boil and steeping the tea long enough. If the old lady got a weak cup of tea or leaves in her cup, there would be the devil to pay. When she peeked into the teapot, the leaves seemed to have settled to the bottom, so she put everything on the tray, after pouring a little milk into a chipped pitcher. The small sugar-bowls were all ready for the trays in the evening. Surveyeing her handiwork, her spirits lifted. Nothing seemed to match, but it did not look too bad.

She found her way through the dim hallway from the kitchen into Mrs. Coghan's untidy parlor. Nothing had been disturbed since she was there before. It was all Mrs. Coghan could do to look after the rest of the house and get the meals. She did not have enough energy left over for her own quarters. Monica found this strangely touching. No wonder the poor woman hit the gin bottle from time to time. She could not have much of a life. She paused for a moment before the photograph of two little boys and smiled faintly. Maybe it was not a dead loss after all. When it came right down to it, Mrs. Coghan had more than she had. The thought was a little depressing.

Unable to knock because of the tray in her hands, she managed to turn the knob and ease her way through the door. Mrs. O'Reilly was sitting up in bed with the dark shawl around her and she gave Monica a toothless grin. She checked herself immediately.

"What the devil have you been up to?" she said in a vinegary voice.

"I made you some tea."

The old woman watched sharply while Monica maneuvered the table into place and set down the tray. With a sigh, she sat down on the edge of the bed.

"Where did you get that crockery?" the old woman asked. "Why, I haven't seen that pot for years. And the old stoneware pitcher! Have you been going through the trash?"

Monica laughed outright. "I thought I'd done very well . . . considering. Wait until you taste the tea."

She began to pour stiffly, careful not to let anything run over the edge of the cups. "This isn't my thing," she confessed, handing the old lady a cup and saucer. "I forgot napkins. You'll have to use the sheet."

The old lady began to laugh, the tea going into commotion in her unsteady hands, and suddenly Monica was laughing with her and she could not seem to stop.

"I'm sorry," she said, putting her cup on the table. "I'm all unstrung. First . . . in my room. And, then, the priest."

"He's mellow today," Mrs. O'Reilly grinned. "Not crocked . . . but he does have a glow on. I don't trust a man unless he drinks and swears. Are they finished with that nonsense yet?"

Monica wiped the moisture from her eyes with the back of her hand. She had not laughed uncontrollably for a long time and she felt better for it. If there is a point at which tension must be released, she had reached that point. She studied the old woman quietly. "Do you believe it's nonsense?" she asked.

"What's here won't go away with a blessing," Mrs. O'Reilly said.

The statement was so matter-of-fact that Monica nodded absently before she realized the enormity of what the old woman had said.

The little face leaned close to her own. "You've felt it, too?"

"What do you mean?" Monica asked carefully. They might not be talking about the same thing at all, and she did not want to get into a conversation that might tip her hand. If she said anything about Mr. Hughes's ideas, it could cause panic, and Mrs. O'Reilly was in no condition for that.

The old woman handed Monica her teacup and wiped her lips petulantly. "That was a good cup of tea. Strong enough to trot a mouse . . . the way it should be. Do you think I'm old and daft?"

"No. You're old but you're very alert."

"Old people get senile, they imagine things. Pour me another cup of tea." The old woman paused thoughtfully. "Promise me you won't tell Peg?"

With a feeling of unreality, Monica lifted the pot. "I won't tell her," she said.

The little eyes peered out of their wrinkles into Monica's face. "I've been lying here thinking about it. Before that, when I was still up and around, I felt it sometimes. But it's stronger now. There's something here besides . . . people."

Monica drew in a deep breath. "What do you think it is?" she asked.

Mrs. O'Reilly shook her head and took a sip of tea. Obviously, she was not alarmed by the thing. "I don't know," she said slowly. "I don't think it's a ghost. It feels different. It acts different, too.

I've seen ghosts . . . that's all you can do: see them. I've been hearing things lately." She brought herself up abruptly. "You won't tell Peg?"

"I won't tell her."

"It's a buzzing sound . . . and talking. I can't understand the words. And one night I thought I heard music. . . ."

"What kind of music?"

"A harp! Maybe I'm hearing the angels already."

"I don't think so," Monica said, putting a reassuring hand on her arm. "A harp's as natural to Ireland as it is to heaven."

"Yes . . . it goes way back. What's here is very old. Have you ever heard of a thin place?"

"I don't know what you mean."

"I heard about it a long time ago. In my village, I think. It's a thin place between the normal world and the supernatural. A kind of door."

"A place in the earth that spirits issue from?"

The old woman shook her head. "Not in the earth. I don't know where it would be. In the air maybe? It's a place where the boundary between us and the spirits isn't thick enough. I think there's one here."

Monica considered this and realized it was what Mr. Hughes thought, too. He had deliberately withheld his view so that it would not influence her. A shiver ran over her skin as though it had been touched by something cold. "You think you're hearing things from . . . the other side?"

Mrs. O'Reilly shrugged her shoulders. "The

other side of what?" she asked earnestly. "Death? I don't think so. No. I really don't. I think . . ."

"Yes?"

"Don't laugh. I think it's more like the fairy world."

An immense relief made Monica release a quiet sigh. She wanted to smile, but controlled herself. "I don't know anything about that," she said.

"I don't either," the old woman said. "I've never believed in it before."

"You believe in the banshee."

"That's different! That's real. I feel something here so strongly and I can't explain it any other way. It's like . . . an earth spirit."

Monica looked at the crucifix on the wall over the old woman's head and back at the shriveled face against the pillows. "Do you believe in things like that?"

"It's asking me to believe."

"You aren't afraid of it." Monica found the thought consoling. "You've lived here all the time, aware of it, but without fear."

"It has nothing to do with me." The thin lips twisted into a little smile. "It gives me something to think about when I'm lying back here all alone. I've figured the whole thing out, I believe. Do you want to hear?"

"Yes, very much."

"The turf shed," the old woman said slowly, "is at the bottom of the whole thing. I think it's an earthwork. Maybe it was a religious place because it was thin."

"Not a tomb?"

"No . . . it was a wall. The end of a wall."

"How do you know that?" Monica asked quickly.

"I don't know how I know. I just do. Can you understand that?"

Monica understood too well, and she did not trust the information. She knew the way perception can dip in and out of time and space to pick up information, and that the information was frequently erroneous or garbled. She was also beginning to realize that the old woman was mildly "afflicted," too. "What about the stone?" she asked. "Do you know anything about that?"

"The stone? Oh, you mean the one in the garden. No. I think one of the monks was a little dotty."

"The stone that was rolled away from Christ's tomb would be potent magic, wouldn't it?"

"Don't let Father MacNeil hear anything like that," the old woman cackled. "The church doesn't like superstition."

"A few hundred years ago, the church wasn't as sophisticated. It even had an exorcism rite. A few hundred years ago, that stone would have been potent magic."

Mrs. O'Reilly considered this for a moment, still smiling. Then she nodded. "Yes. Magic isn't the right word, though. What you're talking about still goes on in the country today. When I was a girl, it was very strong. It's in the people though, not the church. We wore scapulars to keep us healthy and free from harm, but I don't think that was what they were meant for."

Monica thought of the priest going around the house at this moment, sprinkling holy water and "saying a few prayers." She sighed deeply. There was a lot she did not understand. But there was no doubt in her mind, now, that the stone was a talisman of some kind. That it had been put there for the purpose of keeping something away.

"Whatever you're doing," the old woman said suddenly, "be careful. None of us really knows anything, do we? I didn't realize what happened the night you came here. I haven't liked the noises since. It won't bother me. I don't know how I know that, but I do." She worked her lips thoughtfully before she spoke again. "I have a feeling that something . . . happened here . . . long time ago. I don't think the earth spirits were very nice."

It was midafternoon when the men returned. Monica was sunning herself on the front porch, but there did not seem to be much warmth in the sun. She sat cross-legged in her slacks and halter with her manuscript in her lap. She had a motto when she was working: if you can't produce, revise. She had been revising ever since lunchtime and there were marks and additions all over the first half of her paper. She was working on her thesis this afternoon because she had a motto about life: if you can't do anything about something, try to forget it. She had not been very successful with that, either. Her mind kept wandering back to her conversation with Mrs. O'Reilly, and to the peculiar thing that had happened this morning in her room.

Mr. Hughes hailed her from the path below and Tom had to hold him back from running. The old man was panting hard from his climb up the hill and there was a tinge of blue on his lips. Monica waited for the men to reach her, too covered with papers to rise. The loose sheets, stirred by the breeze, were almost blown away and she held some of them down with her foot.

Mr. Hughes sat down heavily on the porch step and Tom watched him with concern while he tried to get his breath. "Are you all right, Evan?" he asked.

The old man waved him aside. "Just too old for that climb. There, that's better!" He gave a deep sigh and the color began to return to his face. "What is it, Monica? What's happened?" he asked, looking at her.

"Nothing," she lied. For some reason, she did not want to tell him about it right now. There would be time enough later. She did not understand it herself enough yet. If she had not talked to Mrs. O'Reilly, she would have convinced herself by now that she had been hallucinating this morning. But now she was not so sure. "You nearly lost your ghost while you were away," she said, attempting to smile.

The old man was alert at once. "What happened?"

"Mrs. Coghan had the house blessed." The men looked at one another quickly. "Oh, you didn't lose him. The house has been like a refrigerator ever since the priest left. I came out here to get warm."

Tom sat down on the step beside Mr. Hughes, stretching his long legs out and leaning on one elbow against the porch near Monica's feet. "Do you have a cigarette?" he asked.

"Smoking again?"

"I need something to hang onto," he said. "Evan . . . you tell her."

She passed a cigarette to Tom and took one herself. Something in Mr. Hughes was communicating itself rapidly to her nervous system and she wanted to be calm when he began.

"We talked about it over lunch," Tom said. "We decided you should know. It isn't pleasant. We didn't want to spoil your holiday."

She did not answer, just stared from one to the other. "I want to know."

"Well," Mr. Hughes began, gripping his thighs with his hands to control his excitement. "I wish you'd been with us. We went to the monastery and the monks were very nice. Something was going on, though . . . I think it was a retreat. They didn't talk much. The monk who saw us was rather young. He didn't make any conversation, just answered the questions he was asked . . . but pleasantly. When he found out that we wanted to look at any old records of the order that were available, he didn't make a bit of fuss. He ushered us into a library, pointed out the records, and left us there alone. I don't think we'd have been so successful if he'd known what was there."

"I'm sure of it," Tom said, "or if he hadn't been keeping silence, perhaps. He probably would have stayed there with us to find the record himself." He looked up at Monica. "We've unearthed an old scandal, my dear."

"Tell me," she said urgently. The papers on her lap tore loose and Tom retrieved them with a smile, stacking them carefully together.

"Corrig *was* a monastery," Mr. Hughes said. "What we thought was impossible was true. It was occupied by a small community of Franciscans a hundred and fifty years ago, while facilities were being built for them elsewhere. The village had no other priests then, and the owner of Corrig . . . our good Mr. Langan, you'll remember, who owned the property at that time . . . donated Corrig temporarily as living quarters and chapel for the priests."

"Legend does die hard," Monica said. "Miss Fay remembered a little of the story."

The old man nodded, gripping his knees until his knuckles went white. "She may have remembered more. Do you recall what she said about her nurse crossing herself when they passed the place . . . that there was something sinister up here? She'd heard the story as a child, I'm sure."

"It frightened her so much, she repressed it," Tom said. "Not an unusual mechanism."

"She hid it so completely she even came here to

live," Mr. Hughes said. "Yet, she'd probably had the whole story from her gabby nurse. . . ."

"Tell me," Monica said urgently.

"I have it all here. I copied it before our young friend returned. Let me read it to you:

> "1 November 1830. Funeral services today for Brother Paul, whose body was discovered this morning in his meditation place by the cave. He left the chapel last night and his absence was not discovered until the brotherhood gathered in the refectory this morning. Major Williams of the British Army was notified. Our brother was interred in the old cemetery in the village. We pray tonight for his eternal soul. *Requiscat in pace*."

"Why did they notify the *army*?" Monica asked.

"Notifying the army was the equivalent of notifying the police then," Tom said. "There weren't even any police in London until about that time."

"Why did they notify anyone? To certify the death?"

"I considered that," Mr. Hughes said. "But it wasn't necessary. I'm sure the rector of the monastery could do that. No . . . they called the army, all right. We went to Dublin Castle and on to headquarters just before lunch."

"It was the most difficult part of the expedition," Tom said. "We nearly ran our feet off before we found what we wanted."

Monica studied the two men with gentle amusement. Tom, tall and rangy, with his quiet sophistication; and Mr. Hughes, small, intense, classically oriented, old, and ill. She was seized with an intense fondness for this unlikely combination of Holmes and Watson. "Surely there weren't any records after such a long time?"

"You're right," Tom smiled, "there weren't. So we went on to the newspaper files and from there to the library. It's been a busy day." He looked at Monica's expectant face and became thoughtful. "You tell her, Evan," he said, turning to extinguish his cigarette.

"All of it?" the old man asked.

"Yes, all of it," Monica answered for Tom. "I'm in this as deeply as you are. Besides, I'm me . . . not Miss Fay."

Mr. Hughes patted her hand and left his in place over it. "Our young monk, Brother Paul," he said softly, "who was so saintly that he meditated by the cave every night . . . was murdered, Monica."

"Who'd do such a thing?"

"You should ask 'How did he do it?' It would answer both questions at once. He was found just outside the cave, almost dismembered. The cross around his neck was torn off so violently that it almost severed his head. The army spent months searching for a lunatic who did not exist. Only the monks suspected part of the truth."

The horror she felt showed on her face.

The old man squeezed her hand tightly. "We told you it wasn't pretty."

"It *was* the monks who erected the stone," she said numbly.

"Undoubtedly. They probably thought the devil himself had got loose from the cave."

"It might have been," Monica said, "we don't know."

"There was something you didn't notice in the monk's account," Mr. Hughes reminded her. He shoved his hastily scribbled notes into her hand. She scanned them briefly and looked at him with a troubled expression on her face. "I don't understand."

"The date," he said. "The first of November. *Semain*."

"The winter festival."

"It should have been dated the second then," Tom said. "The monk was killed at night."

"No," Mr. Hughes said. "I'm sorry, but . . . the Celts divided their calendar differently . . . remember? Nights instead of days. Brother Paul died during the night of the most potent festival of the year. Just as the year was turning to winter when things issue forth from the mounds."

They sat in silence for a few moments. Monica felt a deep disquiet and she knew the others felt the same.

"I think we should call the whole thing off," Tom said suddenly. "This isn't a common, garden-variety ghost. We have to think of Monica."

"It isn't time for the festival now," Mr. Hughes said quickly. "It's only July. Besides, we're prepared for it . . . Brother Paul wasn't. It might have been the odor of his sanctity that enraged the thing."

Monica was hardly listening. The images she had seen from her room that morning were flashing again through her mind. They made more sense now, and she particularly noticed the wall up the hill from where Corrig stood now. "Did the Celts have holy places?" she asked.

Mr. Hughes interrupted his argument at once. "Yes, lots of them. Usually on the top of a hill." He paused thoughtfully. "Each of them was devoted to a tribal god. They built bonfires there on their festivals. You'll recall the story of Patrick defying the high king of Tara at just such a festival, by building his own fire on the Hill of Slane. Other fires weren't permitted, you see. But instead of being killed, he converted the lot of them. Wonderful story . . . but sad. It was the end of the Celts in Ireland."

"What's Bron Trograin?" she asked.

"Where did you get hold of that?"

"I don't know. . . ."

"It means the rage of Trograin. It's an obscure August festival. The real festival was the Lugnasad, in honor of the god, Lug. No one knows who or what Trograin was. An early tribal deity, perhaps . . ."

"An earth spirit?"

Mr. Hughes laughed. "Weren't they all? It depends on how you look at them. Each had his purpose, his anthropomorphic aspect . . . just like the classical gods."

"I want to climb the hill across the road," Monica said suddenly. "Up to the lookout tower."

"This afternoon?" Tom asked.

"Yes . . . now."

He rose to his feet with a gesture of surrender. "If the lady wants to climb the hill, the gentleman must accompany her. We'd ask you, Evan, but I don't think you'd make it."

Monica wanted to protest, to say she intended to go alone, but the situation was awkward.

"I may make it to my bed for a nap," the old man smiled. "It's simply rotten to be old."

"I don't think I agree with you," Tom said. "I think I'd welcome it right now. Providing that age brought with it freedom and peace of mind, of course."

CHAPTER SIX

AN AFTERNOON BREEZE had come up, strong and chilly, and Monica's hair blew across her face and around her neck. Unconsciously, she lifted a hand to brush it out of her eyes. In spite of the cool wind, the walk up the hill began to warm her. She hardly spoke as they took the narrow road between the cottages toward the bare hilltop and the tower. Too much had happened today; thoughts tumbled together in her mind, and her awareness of Tom beside her was another distraction. She remembered the last time she had come down this path. It seemed a long time ago, and she felt no embarrassment about it now. To free herself from an avalanche of impressions, she began to study the neat cottages with their blooming gardens behind their inevitable stone walls. Then she concentrated on the walls alone, massive, always of gray stone, high enough to keep out the stares of strangers unless a gate was left ajar. Every plot of land seemed to be apportioned in Ireland, its ownership marked clearly by the pile of stone around it. Some of the higher walls had chunks of glass stuck into the top of them, as though their owners were withholding a stampede of antelope. This struck her as odd. With the crime rate as low as it was in the country, such precautions were unnecessary. She wondered what basic insecurity in the Irish nature made them construct such barricades.

"I've wanted to talk to you," Tom said.

Her mind appeared to be far away when he spoke to her; actually it was no farther than the nearest wall. She did not answer, because there was nothing to say. She walked quietly at his side for a few moments before he continued. "I couldn't say anything the other day. I was all up in the air. My mind's clearer now."

Her step slowed a little, but she still did not speak.

"There are things you have a right to know. It was all my fault, you see. I let my work get too demanding. I didn't have time for the things she wanted to do. I tried to take her out . . . but it bored me. Small talk is draining. It sticks in my throat." He paused, and when no comment was forthcoming, he said, "I'm probably not a nice person to be married to."

Monica did not reply at once. Something had happened to her: perhaps it was her decision to maintain her space. She knew she loved him, but the feeling was not so urgent. She had acquired patience and a kind of peace. "You and Mr. Hughes have both run away like little boys," she said at last. "Are you really capable of any kind of decision?"

It was Tom who was quiet now. They reached the grassy rise above the cottages and climbed in silence toward the tower. More gray stone, but this time built by the British. Looking out across the water from the hill, she almost expected to see the sails of Napoleon's fleet.

"I think I am," Tom said and, for the first time, she looked at him. "Everything's clearer now . . . I just hadn't made the resolution to carry it out. It was my daughter that really worried me. I told you she was in a boarding school: it's true in a way. She had a serious breakdown brought on by drugs and she's still under medical care. I felt so helpless. We didn't even know what was going on . . . which probably says something for me as a father, too. God, if I had it to do all over again, I'd do everything differently. When I'm free, Monica . . ." But he stopped, still unable to say anything, because he was not free.

Her heart constricted painfully. She walked to the edge of the hill, absently brushing her hair from her face. She did not look at Tom when he joined her. Below, she could make out Corrig and the Chalet, as she had done on their former climb. This time, she knew what she was looking for, and her gaze swept the opposite hillside, trying to eliminate the thick foliage and the dark trees.

"When we were up here before," she said vaguely, "I said something about the Mayan ruins being discovered from the air. Look down at Cor

Hill, just below the entrance to Corrig. Do you see an elevation? Now, follow it to your left, thinking of it as a circle . . ."

There was no doubt about it. The line of the wall was broken now, because of the overgrowth, but it was there, visible because of a slight elevation in the overgrowth and the grass. Tom crouched in an effort to see Cor Hill better. "It looks like an earthwork," he said softly. "I've seen some of them in England. They're easier to make out there, because they're in fields. I think you've made a discovery. . . ."

"It was a wall. Do you see where it ends?"

"At the turf shed. Or of course it might begin there. The way it spirals around the hill . . ."

"In a concentric circle," she said. "From Corrig to the cave."

He rose to his feet, still staring down the hill. "You've broken part of the mystery," he smiled.

"The spiral was on their brooches, too," she said.

"Whose brooches?"

"What do you really think happened to you last night?"

The recollection of last night's encounter brought a change into his eyes. He considered his next words carefully. "I'll tell you the truth," he said at last. "I think something grabbed me by the throat. I know it sounds like nonsense. But I've rejected every other possibility. Something had power enough, energy enough, to try to choke the life out of me."

She gripped the arms of her sweater and hugged herself, shivering slightly. "I think that's what happened, too," she said. "We might all wind up with our heads disconnected from our shoulders."

"We don't have to stay. I really think you should get out of here, Monica. It isn't a game anymore."

She shook her head. "I want to get to the bottom of it, and I'm afraid. I'm all mixed up. Besides, I promised Mr. Hughes."

"Evan will understand. I think you should come to England with me."

Monica's face flushed with anger: she could hardly restrain herself from saying something sharp. Instead, she turned away and started back down the hill, trying to avoid the rocks.

"I didn't mean to offend you," Tom said, following her quickly. "I just meant that I'm going back to England soon and I think you should accompany me on the trip. You can do your research at the British Museum. There must be a copy of every publication in the world there. . . ."

"My grant's for Ireland," Monica said shortly. "What right have you to tell me what to do? I'm frightened, but I don't have to run across the Irish Sea."

"Well, at least get out of the Chalet!" he said with exasperation. "Go back to Dublin to the digs with your Mirish if you please. Anywhere but here."

"He isn't my Mirish!" she said hotly. "Will you

please leave me alone? I've taken care of myself for quite a while . . . I can take care of myself now. I have no intention of leaving the Chalet yet!"

"So be it!" He shrugged his shoulders. "If you stay, then I'm staying, too. I don't trust the mood of the place, Monica. I was an unbeliever, and I've come to that point. There's something more than dangerous there."

"You can go if you like," she said coldly. "I'm not your responsibility. I really don't know what's keeping you on. You say you've made your decisions. There's nothing to keep you from England, then."

She suddenly went silent, wondering at her own vehemence. If she kept talking, she would say something irreparable: better to be silent. She half expected him to stalk down the hill without her, because he was upset, too. Instead, he sighed and looked out over the bay.

"I shall stay on for a short while," he said at last. "I suppose we should see this thing to its conclusion, whatever it is. I only hope to God none of us is killed in the process. I keep thinking about that poor, decapitated monk. Whatever is here is not gentle. I shouldn't be surprised if all hell broke loose. . . ."

They were halfway through their supper when Mr. Hughes, who had had little to say since they entered the dining room, dropped his spoon with a clatter. Monica and Tom looked up in surprise.

"You knew it all along," the old man said to Monica. "You *did* get a telemetric impression from the stone."

"I don't know what you're talking about." She had not told either of them about what had happened during the day, but she had planned to do so immediately after dinner. She still did not know how much she should tell. Mr. Hughes had slept until just before dinner, and he did not know about the wall, either. She was looking forward to telling him about it, and had been about to speak when he dropped his spoon, but his remark about the stone dispelled that notion. He had been quiet because he was dwelling on the information he had turned up in Dublin in the morning. When she said, "I don't know what you're talking about," it was the truth. She had not lost rapport with him, but she had been following the turnings of her own thoughts during the meal, and he had been following his.

"The first time you saw the stone," he prompted, a slow excitement beneath the words. "Don't you remember? You thought of an El Greco painting. A monk praying in front of a cave."

Her pulses fluttered. The picture came back into her mind now. It was not a painting, not El Greco at all. It was like the impressions she had had this morning in her room. Even the colors were the same, that sickly wash of gray and green. There was no distortion in the figure: it was a real man. At the time, her only point of reference had been the Spanish painter. With a sick feeling in her middle she, too, put down her spoon.

"What is it, darling?" Tom asked.

She looked from Mr. Hughes to Tom. His face was concerned and his eyes held hers. For the first time that evening, Mr. Hughes chuckled.

"Forgive me, my dear," he said, "but this is wonderful! I wonder how many clues there have been that we were too stupid to follow?"

"Please, Evan," Tom said, "she's upset."

"I'm all right," Monica said and, to prove it, picked up her spoon again, dipping it carefully into her soup because her hand was trembling. "I was just thinking of what I might have seen. When I was pawing around in the turf shed, for instance." She spooned her soup away from her and her hand was steady when she took it to her lips. "There are a few things you should know. Mrs. O'Reilly has some ideas about what's happening here. She may be sensitive. And I think she's more on the track than we've been."

"That old crone in the back bedroom . . ." Mr. Hughes paused and scratched his beard.

"She's been aware of something for years. She even seems to know we're interested in it. And I can't imagine how she knows, unless . . ."

"Quiet, Mrs. Coghan's coming," the old man said.

He had no sooner spoken than the swinging door from the kitchen opened and Mrs. Coghan entered with a platter of cold lamb. There was a smile on her flushed face, and Monica wondered if it came from having the house blessed. It must be reassuring, she thought, to have faith in a ritual to keep evil away, and she wished that she had some sort of belief to hang onto. She was mildly surprised when Mr. Hughes turned to Mrs. Coghan and said in his most gracious manner, "Is your mother well enough for company this evening?"

Mrs. Coghan was even more surprised. She shut her lips together, glancing at him as she removed the soup dishes and laid the platter of lamb in the middle of the table. She added a bowl of potatoes and a relish dish of mint sauce. "Are you suggesting you'd like to visit her?"

"Exactly. I'll be on my best behavior."

She did not answer him until she had her back to the kitchen door, a tray of dishes hugged to her ample chest. "Sure the two of you would make a fine pair," she said and disappeared into the kitchen.

The men laughed and Monica managed a smile. "You won't upset her?" she asked.

Mr. Hughes shook his head. "I'm a careful man." He passed her the platter and she selected a slice of meat. "Now . . . what did the old hag say?"

"You're incorrigible! She says that, whatever it is, it isn't a ghost. She knows a few and this is something different." Tom smiled and she passed him the tray. "Her idea's bizarre. Have you ever heard of a 'thin place,' Mr. Hughes?"

"A door to the other world. Yes, please go on."

"She's been hearing things. The buzzing, voices, music. A harp, she said. She thinks an earth spirit is causing the disturbances. Something very old and alien to our minds. She said the turf shed's set into a wall. That it was a ritual place."

"The turf shed's a cave."

"She thinks the wall was built around the cave, because the cave is a 'thin place' . . ."

"Monica found the wall today. I was with her," Tom said. "We climbed to the top of the opposite hill and she was able to trace it. There's an earthwork starting just below Corrig that spirals up and around the hill . . . ending in the cave."

The old man dismissed the information with a shrug. "It's impossible," he said. "If it encircled the top of the hill, it would be reasonable. It might have been a fortification at one time. Or a walled city. But what on earth would a wall be doing meandering up the hill? I think you've let your imaginations run away with you . . . at the old woman's suggestion."

"Evan," Tom said softly, "the wall *spirals* up the hill . . . in a concentric circle. Exactly like. . ."

". . . the sign," the old man said wonderingly. "*Cor*. A twisting, a turning. Could it be coincidence?"

Monica sat for six heartbeats, trying to determine how to tell them. Her face flushed and she had to blink her eyes. She wondered how they would take it. Mr. Hughes might say it was her imagination, and Tom . . . what would his diagnosis be? Her heart beat thickly beneath her ribs.

"I . . ." she began, but her voice broke. "I saw the wall this morning. I saw the people, too. They wore brooches with the spiral on them. They were getting ready."

"They were preparing for a festival," Monica replied quietly. "Bron Trograin . . . I think it's soon."

The doorbell rang right after dinner, and Mrs. Coghan ushered Mirish into the living room, where they all sat by the fire. Mr. Hughes looked up with a snort at the interruption, but Monica rose and extended her hands.

"What a nice surprise!" she said warmly, taking Mirish's cold hands in her own. "Here, move in to the fire . . . you're absolutely frozen!"

"When the sun went down, all the heat went with it," Mirish said, holding his hands to the flames. He was clad in an Aran sweater and blue jeans and looked more respectable than he usually did. His wardrobe was small, that of a student subsisting on a small allowance, and he did not care anything about clothes. He had come on the city bus from Dublin, but apparently with the foresight of neatening himself up a bit beforehand. Monica introduced him to her companions, who had only seen him before. Tom was distantly polite, but Mr. Hughes made no secret of his pique over the interruption. They had been deep in discussion and his comfortable pipe was breathing noxious fumes. Monica gave him a look of warning and he altered his mood.

"So, young man, you're a student. What are you studying, if I may ask?" the old man asked. "We're all students of this or that . . . but you're actually in training. Are you interested in literature like Monica?"

"As a matter of fact, sir, I am," Mirish responded, searching Mr. Hughes's face at his tone. "I'm working on my doctorate, too. I hope to teach Celtic literature at Trinity."

The old man's eyes gleamed with sudden interest. "Celtic, is it? Why? The revival of the language in your country has hardly been a smashing success."

"Ah, my interest has nothing to do with that. It's in the manner of antiquities that I'm interested. God knows, we had the language drummed into us in grammar school . . . I did quite well at it, you see. Then, when I got my hands on some of the old manuscripts and found that I could almost read them, the decision was made. You don't think much of Celtic, then?"

"Mr. Hughes is from Wales," Monica put in kindly. "He was raised speaking the language and he's very much interested in the Celts."

"And you?" Mirish asked, looking closely at Tom. "Are you a Celtish dilettante, too?"

"No, indeed," Tom replied politely. "I'm English to the core, only a dull physician."

"Well, it's you who'll be making the money, then," Mirish responded. "Scholars are poor all their lives. But I suppose the National Health has put a stop to that, too?" he asked hopefully. "You're limited to so many patients a year."

"I have all that I can handle . . . and more," Tom said. "That's why I'm on holiday. If you'll excuse me, now, please . . . I must go for my walk."

Mirish nodded, still not taking his gaze from Tom's face. "You better be putting a heavy coat on," he warned. "And some fine, heavy gloves, too."

Tom nodded and left them quickly to go upstairs. There was a moment of silence before Mr. Hughes picked up the previous conversation again.

"What do you think of the possibility of any Celtic high places being this close to Dublin?" the old man asked, leaning eagerly forward in his chair to look into Mirish's face. The young man had fallen into Tom's vacated chair, stretching his toes toward the fire.

"Not likely," he said. "Though, God knows, anything is possible, I suppose. They've been excavating over on the island for years. A few Celtic artifacts have been found. Why do you ask?"

"Just curious," Mr. Hughes said, frowning.

"Well, then," Mirish said, turning to Monica. "How about another look at that bloody stone in the garden, then? It's been on my mind quite a bit. Nothing Celtic about that, I trust?"

"Hardly," Monica smiled. "It's relatively modern. But, do come . . . I'd like to hear your impression of it. Will you excuse us, Mr. Hughes?"

The old man nodded and made a gesture for them to depart with his blessing, trying to conceal his disappointment in the evening. "Perhaps when you're through out there, we can have a little talk," he said as they left.

It was still light outside, a chilly, gray light over the water. Monica led Mirish to the stone and he knelt down to examine it. She watched him closely, but his expression did not change as he read the inscription.

"Ah, well," he said, rising and brushing off his knees. "We Irish are a mad lot, sure enough. God knows what kind of recluse erected this ruddy thing. As to what it means, I suspect that not even God knows."

"Is that all you have to say?"

"Sure, what else is there to say? Someone with a knowledge of the Scriptures—and who in this church-plagued land doesn't have that—went berserk and erected the stone." He hesitated slightly. "Of course, it is rather odd. I wouldn't want to sleep in a house that had a sepulcher nearby. Where is it, do you know?"

"We thought it might have been the turf shed. There's a post and lintel door to the cave. . . ."

"Oh, lovely," he grinned. "It all fits in nicely. It's also just like an Irishman to use a tumulus for turf! Idle, makeshift lot . . ."

Monica shivered. She only had a sweater thrown over her halter top. "Let's go back inside, Mirish. It is chilly out here."

"The Englishman doesn't like me much," he

said as they turned up the path. "The Welshman was even disturbed by my coming . . . why is that?"

"It's just their manner," Monica apologized. "They're really quite nice. . . ."

"Especially the doctor, eh? You're very transparent, girl."

"He's just another guest," Monica said firmly. "I'm very fond of Mr. Hughes, though. I think you'll learn to like him, too. Let's go back and talk to him."

"I'd rather hoped to have an hour alone with you."

"That's quite impossible," Monica smiled. "It's too cold outdoors and there's only one sitting room."

Mirish shrugged. "As you wish. I still say you're transparent."

Tom came out of the door just as they were approaching it and he paused to hold it open for Monica.

"Have a nice walk," she said without enthusiasm and he grunted his affirmation, swathed to the ears in his overcoat.

Mr. Hughes was still waiting by the fire, his red-brown eyes focused on the flames. He stirred and looked up when they entered. "Come over here," he said indicating the empty chairs. "I've a question or two to put to you, young man."

"If I can help at all," Mirish said, falling into the chair again, this time with obvious dejection. Monica felt sorry for him. He had wanted to be with her and was doomed to talk to an old man in whom he had no interest instead.

"The truth is, I haven't any reference books with me . . . and something's been troubling me. What do you know about Bron Trograin?"

"The rage of Trograin, is it? No one knows much. It was celebrated on the first night of August . . . hum, that's tomorrow night, isn't it? It occurred at the same time as the *Lugnasad*, though only the *Lugnasad* is documented. Which probably indicates that Trograin and Lug were two separate deities and one a minor tribal hero. Otherwise, everyone would have been celebrating the *Lugnasad* together on the first night of August. Lug was introduced into Ireland much later than Trograin, supposedly from Gaul, which explains the better documentation . . ."

"Why's the festival called the rage of Trograin?" Monica asked with trepidation.

"Who knows? It goes back so very far," Mirish said. "I don't like the sound of it, do you? Sounds like a regular people-eater, our boy, Trograin. It might have been a sacrificial time."

Monica and Mr. Hughes were very still, the realization of the words striking horror into them. "But it could be something else. . . ." Monica whispered.

"Oh, indeed, it could! As I said, no one knows. Most of the gods were represented with three heads anyway . . . a regular holy trinity. Maybe they have three different moods. That's all I know about them. I'm not much for history unless it's documented, you know."

Mr. Hughes's contented sigh banished the tension in the room. "Tomorrow night," he reflected. "Interesting. Yes, interesting, young man . . ."

Monica walked Mirish to the bus at ten o'clock, wrapped in her heaviest coat, because the fog had come in. As they passed through the quiet village, past the greengrocer's and the pharmacy, housed in wet, gray stone and displaying no lights, Mirish was shivering in his knit sweater, and the fog hung low on the ground when they reached Padraig's Lane and the bus stop.

"When you come to Dublin again, please look in on me," he said while they waited for the empty green double-decker bus to turn on its motor. "It was marvelous when you were living in the digs at town. I miss you a lot."

"Thank you, Mirish. I don't know how long I'll stay out here. It's on a day-to-day basis, right now. We'll have to see how things turn out. . . ."

"What things? The Englishman?"

"No!" she protested, and a little too quickly and hastily added, "Mr. Hughes and I have a sort of project. We have to see how it works out."

"Well, he's old enough not to worry me," Mirish smiled before boarding the bus and hanging onto the pole by the sleepy conductor. "You were right, you know. I liked him once we started to talk. The other one's bad medicine, I think . . . you'd do well to leave him alone."

"Goodnight, Mirish."

"Goodnight, love." He kissed his fingers to her as the bus began to move. "Good luck with your haunted house and all that. . . ."

Monica pushed the collar of her coat up and began to walk on the misty cobbles back through the village. She passed the church and the cemetery, with its Celtic crosses tilted in the mist. A shiver went through her. Brother Paul was buried here. She thought of what Mirish had said about Bron Trograin being tomorrow night: the festival would be a fitting time for some manifestation. But with the fog so thick that she could hardly see her feet, she decided not to think of such things. If the *Guardia*, the police, were on duty, there was no sign of them, though the stationhouse was dimly lit. She was not ordinarily afraid to walk on the streets at night in Ireland, but this sort of night made one think of Jack the Ripper and she picked up her steps to get home as quickly as possible.

She was within two blocks of the Chalet when a mist-shrouded form came into vision, a tall man muffled up so one could not see his face. Her heart went cold. She was thinking of crossing the street, when he said, "Monica? I've come to get you. Evan said you'd walked out on a night like this, and I came to meet you."

Tom. Rather than feeling a relief from anxiety, all her muscles tightened up. She did not want to walk with him, did not want to have anything to do with him. The evening with Mirish had been pleasant and uncomplicated. She wanted to hold on to that. But she had to say something.

"I'm all right, as you can see."

"Yes, but I'm programmed for Britain, and no woman walks out at night there, if she has her senses about her."

"It's just a short way, now. . . ."

He fell into step beside her and she was conscious of his height and a kind of warmth emanating from his body. He made her feel protected and she was not accustomed to feeling that.

"Whatever possessed you to walk to the bus with that boy? I should have thought he would have protested. . . ."

"He didn't think of it any more than I did," she replied. "It was the only way to get a few words together. The Chalet isn't very private."

"Was what you had to say that private?" he ventured, and she did not know what to answer. It occurred to her to tell a lie, to say that what they had to talk about was personal, but she did not stoop to that. Instead, she responded with a question.

"You must be having a relatively lonely stay? Aside from the people at the Chalet, you don't know anyone at all . . . do you?"

"No. But it doesn't bother me. The guests at the Chalet have been amusing enough."

An out-and-out lie. Her face flushed with anger. Of course, she had not really expected him to tell her about the woman at the hotel . . . or had she? A simple explanation that he had a friend in Ireland, who he saw occasionally, would have comforted her somehow. In the face of the lie, she had nothing more to say to him.

They climbed the hill above Corrig in the dark and mist, stumbling on the slippery stone steps. Halfway up, the fog lifted and cleared before they reached the garden of the Chalet. It was almost miraculous, how clear it was up there. Above them, the lights from the house shone warmly and Monica began to walk faster to reach the fireside within.

Tom had no more to say than she did. They entered the door together in silence. She took off her coat and hung it in the hall closet, conscious of Mr. Hughes in his place by the fire.

"Come and have a cup of hot tea," the old man invited. "I had Mrs. Coghan make a pot for you. My goodness, aren't we in a huff now! What happened? Did you have an argument with your young man?"

Monica shot him a glance that silenced him. It was incredible the way Mr. Hughes could pick up emotion, even from across the room. Tom did not join them but, excusing himself, went up the stairs toward his room. The parlor was heavy with the bad feeling between them, and Mr. Hughes picked up on that, too.

"Really, Monica . . . I think you might be nicer to Tom. He's obviously head over heels in love with you."

She burnt her tongue on the tea and replaced the cup in the saucer. "What makes you say that?" she asked evenly.

"I can tell, that's all. And, a short time ago, you were pretty fond of him. What happened?"

"He's married, Mr. Hughes."

"Oh, but not for long. His wife visited him in Dublin last week. She's going to some island for a divorce. She's quite interested in marrying the other chap."

"Are you using your clairvoyance again?" Monica asked, replacing the tea on the table with a shaking hand.

Mr. Hughes laughed. "Not at all. Tom told me about it. His wife got wind of where he was from his call to his daughter. She arranged the whole thing by post."

"What . . . does she look like?"

"I haven't a clue . . . I've never seen a picture. I've a feeling she's red-headed, though."

Had she been so wrong about Tom? And, if all this was true, why had he not told her? She ran the brush through her hair fiercely, uncertain whether to be angry with him or herself. It was probably too late to set things straight between them now. She had behaved abominably tonight: she had not even thanked him for coming out to meet her. And, obviously, he had had no ill intent. She could not understand it, the angry pride that kept her from him. And she could see no way to reconcile things, after her childish behavior. Well, it served her right for getting so entangled to begin with: she usually had better sense.

Once she was ready for bed, something told her not to turn the light off. Outside the window the fog still hung heavy on the road, though stars could be seen twinkling in the black darkness up here. Mr. Hughes was keeping his vigil by the fire: everything was all right. But still, she could not bring herself to turn off the light. Well, there was nothing against sleeping with the light on: she had done it as a child. And obviously, she was not so grown up now.

Though her head was full of speculations and recriminations, she did not know how fast she fell asleep. The next moment of consciousness was in opening her eyes to a new day. A clear, warm day, the last of July, the morning of the festival, she thought at once. Perhaps everything would be over by tonight, one way or another. She would not go through the day without apologizing to Tom. God knew what awaited them by midnight.

She breakfasted alone in the sunny dining room, staring as though mesmerized by the mossy stone. Dr. Jamieson had risen early, Mrs. Coghan said, and Mr. Hughes usually did not rise until noon. After breakfast, Monica wandered the grounds alone, trying to retrace the path she had seen the phantom horses take the day before. No path was in evidence anymore, and she stumbled over roots and got entangled in foliage as she went about her task. If she had not seen it herself from the top of the opposite hill, she would have sworn there never was a path or a wall here.

Perspiring and out of breath, she went to sit by the conservatory at Corrig when she was finished, pausing in the sun for a cigarette and a moment of reflection. It was nearly noon and no sign of Tom yet. She wondered, once again, what she would say to him. This was as awkward as the first time they had met, when she had made the gaff about his profession. Suddenly she realized that she had not been tuning in on anyone since the vision the previous morning. It was almost as though all her energy had been drained. Yes, something was different in her. For one thing, she was no longer afraid, almost as though she were on the side of the phantoms. But that was ridiculous. She had been preoccupied, that was all. The vision and the house blessing had taken quite a bit out of her, and this trek up the hill this morning did not leave much intact. There was nothing like good physical exercise to banish goblins. Or was it, after all, the news Mr. Hughes had given her last night?

Her nerves were alerted when she heard a sound in the brush and she turned her full attention on the dark green foliage surrounding the conservatory at the other side of the wall. Whatever it was, it was too large to be a bird, and there were few small animals about. For a moment, apprehension came back to her. Then, the bushes parted and Tom stepped through, followed by a large black dog.

"Oh," he said. "Hello. I didn't expect to find anyone here."

"Who's your friend?" she asked.

"Damned if I know. I met him on the way over here. Fierce-looking fellow, isn't he? No breed that I know."

Monica stared with fascination at the dog's unusual face, broad across the forehead and nose, the eyes too far apart, not friendly at all. Amber eyes. Most peculiar, yet she had seen his like somewhere before.

"He seems docile enough," she remarked, but she did not put her hand out to stroke the broad muzzle. "Have I taken your place?"

"No . . . not at all. I do come here sometimes to sit. It's a wild place, isn't it?"

"Mr. Hughes brought me here the first day I came. Yes, it's wild and overgrown, and . . ." She looked into his face and his gaze met hers. She did not know what to say.

"What is it, Monica? We haven't been friends at all for the past few days, and you've a searching look in your face."

"Oh, Tom . . . I got all mixed up."

"Why?"

"I've drawn some wrong conclusions. My ESP isn't working well."

He sat down on the bench beside her, and the dog remained standing, staring at them with his short ears rigid. Monica did not like the look of the animal; yet, it was strangely familiar. Where had she seen a dog like that?

Tom took her hand in his and smiled faintly. "Tell me about it."

"It doesn't matter, now. Tom! Look at him!"

The dog's lip had curled back in a silent snarl, baring sharp, pointed teeth. A feeling of terror overcame Monica and she clung to Tom's hand. He put his other hand over hers.

"He isn't so fierce," he consoled her. "There hasn't been a sound out of him. He's just showing off . . . I think."

"Maybe he's mad. As soon as you sat down, he began to snarl. Can't you get rid of him?"

Tom let go of her hand and rose to his feet. He picked up a stone and hurled it into the foliage, expecting the dog to fetch and carry, but the animal did not move, though he began to pant and the teeth were no longer visible.

"Come on, boy . . . beat it!" Tom commanded. "I didn't know you were going to get ugly when you started to follow me. Get!"

But the dog held his position with his golden eyes fixed on Monica's face. Suddenly, without knowing why, she said in a soft voice, "Go home."

The words worked like magic: the dog disappeared into the bushes. Both she and Tom were surprised, and Monica gave a shudder.

"That's a terrible animal!" she muttered. "And I've seen him somewhere. . . ."

"He probably runs the grounds. Well, he seems to have vanished, now. He responded to the soft touch . . . or do you have a way with dogs?"

Tom reclaimed his seat beside her, but he did

not take her hand again. Instead, he stared around him, at the spot of sun in which they were sitting, glinting on the strewn glass of the conservatory and at the overgrown plants, stretching their leaves out of the broken windows.

"I'd like to tell you something," he said. "I couldn't before. . . ."

Monica waited tensely, with her hands clasped tightly in her lap.

"Everything's settled back in England. My wife's filing for the divorce. It's all going to be all right, after all. I . . ." he sighed and turned his gaze full upon her. "Are you serious about that Irish boy?"

Monica smiled slightly. They were both feeling each other out, with the tension mounting. "Mirish is nice. But I could never be more than a good friend to him."

"Is there anyone else?"

She shook her head and he smiled a little, too.

"What do you say we start all over? Something went wrong somewhere. Monica, I . . . think I love you."

"You *think*?"

"Well, I try to look at things reasonably and we haven't known each other long. I *do* love you . . . but perhaps you're too young for me . . ."

"That's something I should decide," she said, extending her hand to him. He had her in his arms immediately.

"Then, it's all right?" he asked.

But before she could answer, his lips were on

hers, kissing her gently and, then, with increasing demand. She drew back, breathless.

"Tom . . . I've wanted this. I love you so much."

And they were kissing again, so intent on their communion that they did not hear the sound at once. Only slowly did it penetrate their passion, a low, fierce snarl that made them both draw apart.

"It's that dog," Monica whispered. "He's watching us from somewhere. . . . It sounded just like that sound in the living room that night, before . . . you were attacked."

"I was thinking the same thing. Come, let's get out of here. I know there's nothing ghostly about that animal. I'll kick him in the face if he comes near us."

Silently, they made their way to the dark, overgrown gray wall between Corrig and the Chalet. Tom helped Monica climb over and they walked quickly toward the guest house, so fast that Monica did not have time to peer into the shrubbery around them.

Only when they were safe on the porch did a recollection begin to dawn in the back of her brain. Clasping Tom's hand tightly in her cold one, she whispered, "I know where I saw him."

"Who?"

"That dog . . . or one very like him. It was in the procession coming up the hill. It was a mastiff . . . a war hound, Tom!"

* * *

The hearthstone was still bare at midnight, but none of them made a move to go up to their rooms, and Monica wondered sleepily if it was because there was companionship in the parlor by the fire. Ever since Mr. Hughes had returned from his second visit to Mrs. O'Reilly, they had sat there together, drinking coffee and smoking, indulging only in desultory conversation. Mr. Hughes had lit his pipe so many times that the ashtray at his elbow was nearly full of burnt matches. He was attempting to light it again now, but his mind was not really on it, and he added a few more curled matches to the pile, drawing abstractedly and fruitlessly on the stem.

"The spiral's used in witchcraft, too," he observed mildly, as though voicing his thoughts to himself. "It has no beginning and no end. There aren't any animals in the house, are there?"

Monica's heart picked up a beat. "No," she said. "Why . . . did you hear something? I'd hate to think that dog was still around."

He shook his head slowly and gave a short grunt. "Just considering all the possibilities. My talks with Mrs. O'Reilly unnerved me. I have a horror of weird old women, you see."

Monica relaxed. She was even tired enough to find the idea amusing. By the clock on the mantel, it was almost one o'clock. She glanced fondly at Tom, and he winked at her, weariness etched in every line of his face. Though he had not spoken for some time, he seemed prepared to remain as long as they did.

"Maybe you really fixed it," Monica said to Mr. Hughes. "The cross on the circle bit. Or maybe the priest . . ."

"Maybe," the old man said. "And I have the feeling that tonight is our last chance. Everything seems to have been leading to the festival of Bron Trograin. Unless something happens tonight, I have the feeling it won't happen at all."

"Mrs. O'Reilly will have to carry on alone," Monica said.

He shuddered and wheezed a laugh. "She frightens me. She's so convinced about what is here. And she's so near to dying, she's almost dipping over the edge."

"She's always been like that, I suspect. She's never questioned her talent or that she's a little different. She's just accepted it as a natural gift."

"Yes, and delighted in it, I'll wager. She informed me tonight that she has her power because she's the seventh daughter of a seventh daughter and was born at night!"

"I wonder where superstition ends in these things . . . and science begins?" Monica smiled. "Was she also born with a caul?"

"She neglected to tell me," Mr. Hughes smiled, "but she told me about that damned banshee. I still have gooseflesh on my arms."

"What else did she have to say?" Tom asked, smiling lazily.

The old man hesitated, fidgeting with his pipe. He put it in his pocket and took it out again, almost at once, moving it from one hand to the other. Finally he decided to clean it, and produced a small ream from his pocket. "She thinks Monica's the focus of the disturbance," he said evasively.

Tom laughed. "You've thought that all along. She just picked up your thought and handed it back to you, because that was what you wanted to hear."

"Maybe," Mr. Hughes considered. "She added a few embellishments, though."

"Well?"

"Well. All right. It's too late to matter. It goes back to the old woman's earlier questions, which amused you both so much. She says Monica's . . . er . . . unmarried state . . . makes her especially potent in this situation. That and a certain life force and freedom of spirit. And, of course, the fact that she can communicate. She says, further, that it would be better for Monica if she got out of this house. But that's taken care of already." He turned to Monica. "Are you a horsewoman, my dear?"

She was mildly surprised. "What has that to do with it? Yes. Not your English saddle type, of course . . . but I love to ride."

"That's what she said." The old man shook his head slowly. "She had an image of you on horseback. I hope you hadn't told her about it?"

"No . . . she beamed right in on that one," Monica admitted. "Did I tell you those people this morning had horses? With bronze trappings. I wish it had been clearer. The whole thing was hazy and washed with grayish-green light."

"I'd have given anything in the world to see it," Mr. Hughes said forcefully. "So near . . . and yet so far . . . so very far." His eyes went dreamy and he took out his tobacco pouch. "I think what you saw was the preparations for the festival of Bron Trograin, if not the actual thing."

"I wonder why the festival was called the rage of Trograin . . . it sounds ominous."

"No one knows. It was just too long ago," the old man said. "By the way, where did you get hold of Bron Trograin? Have you been doing a little research of your own? You said you didn't hear anything when the images appeared."

Monica considered this for a moment: it was true. She recalled the stony silence that descended during her vision. She had likened in her mind to being deaf. "No. I haven't read anything," she said. "It just popped into my head. Later . . . when I was talking to you."

Their glances met and held. A slow smile began to light Mr. Hughes's face; the gold crown on his tooth flashed in the firelight. Monica nodded slowly and they both began to laugh.

"Would you mind letting me in on this?" Tom said. "I hate to intrude upon your mental conversation, but . . ."

Monica shook her head back and forth, still laughing. "I picked his mind," she said.

"You what?"

Monica yawned. "We're probably low on energy."

"You make us sound like batteries," Mr. Hughes snapped. Tom smiled wearily and looked at Monica fondly, through half-closed eyes. This was not lost on the old man and his face grew speculative. "I think you've messed things up," he said to Tom.

"*I* have. I'm just the innocent bystander."

"You were the rival," Mr. Hughes said. "You've won. It's as simple as that."

Monica touched the old man gently on the sleeve. "Maybe it wasn't meant to go any further," she said. "Maybe by deciphering the sign . . . its sign . . . we accomplished all that was expected of us."

"What have we learned?" Mr. Hughes asked absently. "That the sign was a symbol of a wall . . . a place . . . a tribe? Why would it want us to know that?"

"It might also have been the symbol of an entity," Tom suggested. "The sign for *ego*. 'I am.'"

"Possible," the old man said. "Entirely possible. A card of introduction, so to speak. I don't think there's a case on record in which a real manifestation made any sense. It doesn't feel right, though. I wish we had more time."

"I'm sorry," Monica said.

Mr. Hughes put his hand over hers and stared into the dying coals in the grate. "I guess this *is* it."

"Are you staying on?"

He nodded vaguely. "For a while, I guess. We

were so close, Monica. I wish I could have seen it. I'd give my life to know what it is."

"I thought you were pretty sure," Tom said.

"Everything pointed that way. It's power's like ours, though . . . inconsistent. It dims and brightens like a light bulb. Even that explains something, though. Why there are disturbances in a house for a while, and then the house seems 'well' again."

"It also proves there's something on the other side," Monica mused. "I suspect I'll be spending a little time reconstructing my views."

"I suppose you'll be leaving?" the old man asked.

"Yes, I guess so. There are still six months left on my grant, and I still have my paper to write. But I'll be here longer than that."

"Well, I suppose we should consider ourselves fortunate. We've experienced more than a lot of people do. Maybe we aren't ready yet for anything more." The old man was silent for a moment, then he added stubbornly, "I wish I could have seen it!"

Monica stirred in her sleep. A slight noise reached her consciousness, like the clicking of the latch on the door, and she opened her eyes in the darkness. There was someone in her room, but she was not frightened. The presence in the dark was friendly and the room was warm. Sleep-disoriented, she tried to focus her eyes. "Darling?" she asked sleepily.

He knelt beside her bed in silence and began to caress her hair. She understood. They did not know when they would see each other again: he would be leaving for England soon. And, in the dead of night, alone in his room, he could not stay away from her. He had come to her now, quietly, almost apologetically, to be near her, to make her his own. With a sudden rush of love, she reached her arms out to embrace him. He came to them quickly, murmuring against her neck, and she caressed his naked shoulders, her hands admiring their width and strength.

"Darling," she said and felt the sweetness of his breath as he murmured her name. His lips brushed her face, her neck, her hair, and she longed for him to kiss her. Instead, he tantalized her with his whispering and the gentle exploration of his mouth.

"Oh, Tom," she cried.

Coldness filled the room like a blast of wind off a glacier. The form in her arms turned to ice. Terror set in so intensely that she could not move. Its icy electricity seemed to jump from the walls. She knew she would die if it did not release her: it was like being embraced by a corpse. She struggled feebly, unable to extricate herself from the weight, a scream frozen in her throat.

"Go away!" she managed to whisper, and a humming sound filled the room, like the rage of swarming bees, tuned exactly to the wavelength of her nerves. As it grew louder, Lyn flashed through her mind, and with a tremendous effort, she finally managed to scream. Once the vacuum of horror was released, she screamed and screamed to drown out the angry humming in her ears. Suddenly the weight of her breast grew lighter, the form in her arms dissolving like a dream. When the light went on, she was sobbing hysterically.

She recoiled when Tom tried to embrace her, but he was gently insistent, and his arms were warm and familiar. She clung to him desperately, still sobbing and trembling with shock.

"It's all right, darling," he said softly. "It's all right. It's out now. You woke me just in time."

They were like the words she had heard in the darkness; they made no sense to her at all. Tom wrapped a sweater around her bare shoulders and rubbed her hands to make them warm. "Hop back into bed, now. Under the covers. You're a little shaky. I'll get you some hot tea."

"No . . . don't go!"

Mr. Hughes walked into the room, fully clothed, and stopped abruptly when he saw her face. "You're white as a sheet. It's all right, now. It's completely out. Are you all right, Monica?"

"She's nearly out of her head with fear."

"I don't wonder. You can thank her for your life. How did you know, Monica? Was it a dream?"

She shook her head mutely from side to side. The whole thing came back to her and she hid her face in her hands. *"I thought it was you!"*

"It was, darling. My bed was like a pyre when your screams finally reached me."

She tried to collect her thoughts. "What? I don't understand. . . ."

"His bed caught fire," Mr. Hughes said. "Your screams wakened him. You must have gone to bed with a cigarette, Tom."

"I wasn't smoking. Monica, look at me. If you didn't know about the bed . . . what made you scream?"

She lay back against the pillows, looking at them blank-faced. Somewhere just below her larynx, she felt the coldness of the scream rising again, and she tried to hold it down. Mrs. Coghan appeared at the door in an old robe and curlers, her face puffy with sleep. "I smell smoke," she said. "Are you all right, Miss Rudloe?"

Mr. Hughes toddled to the door and put an arm around her shoulders to lead her out of the room. "It's all right," he said. "There was a little fire, but it's out now. Don't worry about a thing. We'll take care of the damage."

Tom looked down at Monica's hands and tightened his own around them. "They're still cold," he said. "The whole room is."

She turned her head away from him. "It was here."

"Did you see it?"

She shook her head and stared out the window. "The mist is here again."

"The full treatment," he said bitterly, "with a few variations."

"Tom, I feel . . ." Tears welled up in her eyes. "I didn't know who it was. I sensed so much . . . affection. Oh, Tom, I thought it was you! I welcomed the embraces of that . . . thing."

His hands held hers tightly. They were strong and sure. "You thought I'd come to your room? Don't we have an agreement?"

"What I sensed could only have been you," she said urgently. "It didn't reveal itself until I called you by name. Then it . . ." She shuddered and tears streaked down her face. "I'm so ashamed."

He kissed her gently on the lips. "It was a trick. No one's touched you. And no one's going to, either, until things are right. I love you."

Mr. Hughes knocked on the open door and came into the room just as they were embracing. "I beg your pardon," he said, turning to leave.

"Come in, Evan," Tom said. "Did you get Mrs. Coghan settled?"

"She's tearing the whole bed apart and making it up again," the old man said, looking around him. He took the chair from Monica's typing table and set it beside the bed. "That bed looks like it went up by spontaneous combustion, Tom. You were damn lucky to get away without any burns."

"Your bed," Monica said. "It didn't penetrate . . ."

"I told you," Tom said, "your screams woke me just as the bed burst into flames. You were still screaming while we were putting it out. Evan came up immediately. We thought your screams were connected with the fire."

"It happened when it got angry," Monica said. "It happened when I called your name!"

Mr. Hughes was immediately alert. "It *was* here, then? I noticed the coldness and the mist. . . ."

"It was here," Monica said. "No wonder I couldn't understand what it was saying. When I called Tom's name, all the warmth left, and the humming sound began. Just like with Lyn that night. When I began screaming, it dissolved and went away."

"Well, at least we know where the warmth went," Tom said, but Mr. Hughes was no longer listening.

"The primitive cunning of it. The pieces are all in place, now, aren't they? I'm glad you're both leaving tomorrow. This thing's dangerous after all. I think if Monica hadn't screamed, she would have died. It's been determined from the very beginning to take her back with it."

"Back . . . where?"

"To the *orbis aulius* from whence it came. In Irish legend, all graves and tumuli give entrance to it. The earth wall and turf shed are a tumulus, I think. Mrs. O'Reilly may be right. We've found the thin place between two worlds quite by accident."

"The *orbis aulius*?" Monica asked.

"The other world," Tom said, "in which none of us have believed."

"But why *me*? Because it can reach me through my mind?"

The old man considered this silently. At last, he said, "Probably. But not altogether, I think." He paused uncomfortably. "What do you think about reincarnation?"

"It isn't my bag," Monica said, without hesitation. "But, then, none of this is."

"I wish I could be as certain as you are," Mr. Hughes said. "I've always suspected I'm a reincarnated Celt."

"Are you serious?" Tom asked.

"Not really, I suppose. It's just that I have such an affinity for those misty, ancient people. When I read their poetry or look at their craftsmanship, it's more like recalling than learning. I'm in harmony with them. Of course, speaking Gaelic as my native tongue . . ." He looked at Monica suddenly. "Did it say anything tonight?"

"Yes." A shiver ran through her and she tightened her lips. "It was murmuring all the time. I can't tell you what it said, though. Except for my name. It knew my name."

"Hm," the old man said. "That means it can communicate and hear us. There is some contact after all." He looked thoughtfully toward the windowpane, beading moisture from the mist outside. "Your room is warm now, but we still have the fog." He rose with sudden decision. "I think you should get some sleep."

"I'm staying up," Monica said with decision, then, more softly, to Tom: "There are a lot of things I have to sort out in my mind."

"I don't expect any of us will sleep much," he

agreed with a faint smile. "Actually, it might be a good idea to write everything down before we begin to exaggerate." He paused thoughtfully, staring at his hands, and then turned to Mr. Hughes. "I'm going to follow up your suggestion, Evan. After what's happened here . . . well, the whole subject wants investigating, doesn't it?" Gripping Monica's hand, he gently scrutinized her face. "Does it sound like any kind of life to you? I'd have to cut back on my practice. . . ."

She found her mind curiously divided between what was happening now and what had taken place such a short time ago, and a feeling of unreality and disorientation seized her. She knew instinctively that if she committed herself to Tom and a life of this kind of investigation, things of a similar nature might occur, and the thought made her shudder. But, weighing the man against his proposal, there was only one choice to be made. Her voice was steady when she answered, "I don't see how we can do anything else."

"Splendid, splendid," Mr. Hughes said, staring abstractedly at the window. "I wish you both the best of luck. And if I don't see you before you leave in the morning, I want you to know it's been . . . splendid." His smile was almost wistful when he turned to go. "The evening wasn't so dull after all. Good-bye."

The mist was dispersing a little, leaving only a few strands for the moon to chase, when Monica moved the typewriter from the little table, pulled the chair back into place, and started to write. The fear had passed now, but her mind was a welter of impressions, what had happened earlier confused in some way with her love for Tom. Aside from his suggestion that she should write everything down before she got fanciful, she really wanted to do it. It might clear her thoughts. The bright yellow light from the lamp and the warmth of the room had given her confidence to send him to his own room. Right now, she wanted more than anything else to be alone.

Because, from an early age, she had been ruthlessly honest with herself, even when the hard light of truth made her wince, it did not take her long to analyze what was bothering her. With the realization, she hesitated a moment, wondering how she should put it down. Then, almost recklessly, she threw caution aside and wrote everything just the way it had happened. If Tom was the man she thought he was, he would understand. If they were to spend their lives investigating such phenomena, they would have to be honest. Otherwise their studies would have no validity. Conscious of the fact that her own emotions might have precipitated the experience, she wrote rapidly, hardly pausing for punctuation, describing in detail the indefinable sweetness of the manifestation in her arms before it turned to icy terror, the primitive outpouring of unrestrained desire . . . and the response it brought in her. The guilt she had felt earlier was due, not so much to the fact that someone besides Tom had embraced her, but to the fact that she had responded in turn.

When she looked up from her table, the mist was gone, and she felt a vague nostalgia running side by side with her relief. How could anything so fully tender possess such violence? How could a being that had caressed her so gently turn to icy rage and destruction at the very mention of another man's name? Suddenly, desperately, she wanted to talk to Mr. Hughes. And at the thought of him, something skittered to the top of her consciousness, not to nudge and nibble, but fully armed with teeth.

The old man's exit from the room had been peculiar: it was unlike him. At the time, she had been only slightly aware of the trite words and the way he stared vaguely at the mist outside the window, saying "Splendid, splendid," instead of rejoicing as he should have over Tom's decision to go into research. And his hasty good-bye. Surely, they were close enough for him to rise to see them off in the morning. . . .

Without pausing to put on a robe, she crept into the hallway, the cardigan still flung over her shoulders, and paused briefly before Mr. Hughes's door. She did not open it, she knew no one was inside. She sensed Tom's presence in the odor of fire as she passed his room. He had opened a window and a cool breeze blew beneath the door on her bare feet. She decided not to bother him. It might only be her imagination, she could never tell. She might find Mr. Hughes in his usual place by the fire, snoring contentedly. But she did not think so. There were too many unanswered questions in her mind for him to ignore them . . . his interest was more passionate than hers.

At the foot of the stairs, in the darkness, a sound reached her that made her cling to the balustrade. A high, plaintive, keening wail came from the rear of the house. She hesitated only a moment, to locate it better, and moved through the dining room and dark kitchen, feeling her way through the pantry hall to Mrs. Coghan's quarters. It did not enter her mind to knock. Mrs. Coghan's bedroom door was closed; she had no doubt fallen into a heavy sleep when she finally got back to bed. The sound was coming from Mrs. O'Reilly's room.

Opening the door cautiously, her hand went numb on the doorknob. In the moonlight beside the bed, a shrouded figure was swaying and keening the indescribable wail. Her fingers hardly felt the wall as she moved them silently to the light switch. A cry tore through her throat at what she saw: an eerie figure, swathed in a sheet, sat in the cane chair, rocking back and forth. The keening ceased at once.

"It's so cold," Mrs. O'Reilly complained from the folds of the sheet. "Every bone in me body aches!"

Monica exhaled the breath she had drawn when she entered the room. Her knees were trembling a little when she went over to stoke up the fire. "What the devil are you doing out of bed?" she asked sharply, as a reaction to her fright. "I didn't think you could move. . . ."

"It was that or freeze to death," the old woman said petulantly, pulling the sheet around her. "Peg didn't hear me when I called."

The poor old soul, Monica thought ruefully, half amused, now, at her reaction to the "apparition." She threw some coal on the fire and braced a few blocks of turf against it so there would be enough ventilation for it to ignite.

"Aren't you cold?" the old woman asked, observing Monica's bare feet and nightgown. Monica shook her head slowly; for the second time tonight, she had not felt the cold. "It started when the old man went into the turf shed," Mrs. O'Reilly added.

"Into the turf shed? When?"

"After Peg came down. I heard him in the kitchen and saw his light in the fog. Where are you going? Come back here . . . I'm freezing to death!"

Almost without touching the ground, Monica's bare feet carried her back through the pantries and the kitchen and through the door into the garden, where they were lost in the low fog still hanging on the ground. A faint light emitted from the turf shed and she approached it carefully, ignoring the stones on the path cutting her feet, her mind full of Brother Paul. A terrible physical weariness overcame her. One fright after another had sapped her energy, and her adrenals begged for respite, urging her to lie down right there in the fog on the path, and go to sleep. By the time she reached the door of the turf shed, her senses were so dulled that she was prepared for anything but what she saw.

Mr. Hughes stood inside the cave with the fog swirling to his knees, his flashlight directed on a misty spot in the far wall. She was ready to speak his name when she noticed that the place on which the light played was darker in the center, as though, somehow, a door had opened in the mist. Unaware of her presence, the old man was speaking rapidly in a fluid, guttural tongue, his whole attention riveted on the dark opening. She tensed all over when she heard something answer him in a babbling murmur.

Frozen to the spot just inside the door, she whispered, "What is it?"

Without turning around, Mr. Hughes said, "Quiet . . . quiet."

"It spoke to you," she insisted woodenly, and he nodded, playing his light on the opening.

"The Gaelic's different. Irish . . . a very archaic form," he said softly. "It's like trying to speak modern English to Beowulf, but I can make out some of it. There was a woman. He lost her. Something about a battle. He didn't like the house blessing. He doesn't like Christians. . . . Look!"

A pale light twisted dimly in the center of the opening, swirling, attempting to take form. Monica moved swiftly into the cave and stood behind

Mr. Hughes, her cold hands grasping the rough tweed of his jacket.

"The thin place is open," he said. "It's been that way for an hour. But it was your coming here that did this. . . ."

A vague form took shape before them, blurring and moving, gray, green, and bronze, like an oversoaked color transparency.

"Stay close behind me," the old man said. "Be prepared to leave if you have to."

The cave was warm enough, she was not frightened. Rather, she watched the scene before her with a detached fascination, with no thought of her own personal safety entering into it, as though it were a dream.

"Monica," the old man said eagerly, "help him come."

She hesitated momentarily, and it was almost fatal. The light lost what form it had and dimmed perceptibly.

"Monica!"

At Mr. Hughes's command, she drew in her breath with half-closed eyes, letting go of her mind as she had wanted to since coming outdoors. It came back, slowly at first, and then encouraged by her, surrended. It materialized, drenched in bronze and green, an image floating on water. The form was that of a man, but it could not hold its shape. Mr. Hughes drew in a wheezing breath as it changed subtly from an angular, high-cheekboned youth to the form of a mature male . . . tall, strong, golden-haired, a dark homespun cloak covering one side of his naked body. Before she could discern the design on the shoulder brooch, the shape shifted again. A cripple stood before them, bleeding, mutilated, missing one eye, a concentration of malignant energy and wrath in the eye that remained. She gripped her fingers into Mr. Hughes's shoulders. He must have had the same thought, because he addressed a question to the figure. The answering—fluid babble—did not pass through the lips of the figure, but came from all around them. Monica caught only one word: *fear*. The shape dissolved again.

"I'm not afraid," she said quietly to Mr. Hughes. "Are you?"

"*Fear* is the pronunciation of the word for 'man,'" he said tightly. "He says he is all of these . . . a man."

"All the forms he had in life," she marveled softly. "But what . . ."

The manifestation held briefly in the dark hole in the mist, and a gold-maned warrior stood there arrogantly, his weight thrown back on one foot, surveying them narrowly. The face was beautiful. Monica moved out from behind Mr. Hughes to see him better. The bold cheekbones and finely modeled lips were strong and proud, without cruelty: the shoulders might have been those of a statue.

"The primal strain," the old man whispered. "Danubian. Magnificent!"

But even as he spoke, the narrow eyes focused on Monica with an expression of tenderness and, almost violently, another metamorphosis began.

Stunned by the moment of recognition, she could hardly get her breath. Her heart beat painfully. The temperature of the cave fell, and the flashlight wavered in Mr. Hughes's fingers. He gripped it tightly with both hands to steady it. Frightened by the sudden change which carried with it a feeling of foreboding, Monica tried to regain control of the situation by withdrawing her attention. It was too late: the manifestation had the ascendency. They both drew back at the same time when the eyeless, mutilated face materialized in the darkness, with an ugly smile on its twisted lips. In a flash of intuition, Monica read the whole story in the figure and tried to pull Mr. Hughes to the door.

"He went insane," she said stiffly. "He's all these people, but he died insane!"

The mist thickened, until it surrounded them completely, and a strange odor came with it which made Monica gasp and Mr. Hughes cry out in disgust and drop his light. A smell of mold and blood assailed their nostrils, shaking their nerve completely, and Mr. Hughes cried out, "Run! The stone in the garden . . . it's your only hope!" And he began speaking loudly in an incomprehensible tongue. "Trograin . . ."

The cold and the odor of death constricted Monica's chest like strong arms: she was unable to breathe. In blind panic, she stumbled out of the turf shed, gulping great gasps of air. A cruel hand was crushing her heart like a savage fist and the odor clung to her. The pebbles of the path cut into her feet as she rushed through the mist toward the protection of the sentinel stone, and threw her arms wildly around its mossy surface, breathing a prayer. A flash of green light made the stone tremble beneath her body and darkness enfolded her like a moldy homespun cloak.

"I liked him so much. I never did tell him so."
She was on the couch in the parlor and dawn was in the window, glimmering gray, a few stars still showing through. Tom was dressing her forehead while Mrs. Coghan stood by, handing him cotton swabs dipped in antiseptic. The sting of the alcohol on the open wound felt good: it told her she was still alive. She breathed in the fumes, desperately, with streaming eyes to dispel the other smell.

"You didn't have to tell him," Tom said gently. "He knew. You should have a suture. Mrs. Coghan, a butterfly, please."

Her face worn, still in curlers, Mrs. Coghan responded automatically to the order, pulling off a short length of adhesive and cutting it carefully. "I was afraid this would happen," she said mournfully. "He had a bad heart. Oh, God in heaven, he was such a nice man. The ambulance will be here soon, Doctor. That damn path! I'm going to get rid of this place. . . ."

"Don't do anything impulsive," Tom said coolly, as he placed the bandage with one hand, pressing the flaps of skin together with his fingers. "There . . . it'll be all right, darling. You may have a little scar." He kissed her briefly on the lips. "I must get in touch with Evan's son, now."

"Do you have his address?"

"Yes. There was a letter addressed to Rome and forwarded here."

Monica smiled bleakly, brushing the tears away with the back of her hand. "You didn't know about his little game? A mailing service. His son thinks he's on the continent. It amused Mr. Hughes . . . made him feel like a runaway." Tears stung her eyes again. She clasped Tom's hand and pulled him close to her. "Was he all right? It wasn't like . . . Brother Paul?"

"It was a heart attack," he said, but his gray eyes searched hers. "What were you doing out there?"

She relinquished his hand reluctantly. "Later. After you call Mr. Hughes's son." She watched Mrs. Coghan gather up the balls of cotton on a tray. She moved heavily, wearily, and Monica felt a twinge of pain for her.

"You didn't really mean it . . . about selling the house?"

Mrs. Coghan shook her head. "They've been talking about making a hotel out of Corrig. They want my property, but I wouldn't sell it, Miss Rudloe. Even if there's something wrong with the place . . . well, it's mine. That poor old man. And mother will be next, I'm thinking. It'll be a flaming miracle if they don't slide all the way down the hill with that stretcher."

Monica was thoughtful a moment. "Don't ever remove the stone," she said at last.

"The lightning almost did it for me," Mrs. Coghan said indifferently. "I'll go get you a strong cup of tea. You look peaky."

She already had her things together and was leaving the room before Monica was alert enough to pursue the subject. Tom held the swinging door for Mrs. Coghan as she went into the kitchen, and his face was thoughtful when he returned to the parlor. She made room for him to sit down beside her on the couch and he took her hand.

"I thought you said Ian Hughes didn't know where his father was?" he said.

"He didn't. Mr. Hughes told me all about it."

"Evan underrated his son, then. He knew he was in Ireland. He knew he was dead, too." He paused with a frown. "He said he was waiting for my call. . . ."

They stared at each other for a moment and Monica's fingers twisted into the afghan over her knees. "Tom . . ."

He shrugged. Then he smiled grimly. "Maybe it's hereditary. We'll have to look him up . . . I was going to anyway. Look, darling, I don't know what happened out there last night, but I want to get you away from here today. I'll pack your bags."

"There isn't any danger now. It's gone. The house is clean."

"How can we be sure? It's gone undercover before."

"It's gone," she repeated with conviction. "Mr. Hughes's death broke the communication . . . or his sacrifice propitiated it for a while . . ."

"Sacrifice?"

She nodded sadly, too weary for any more tears. "He gave his life to save me. He tried to buy time to get me to the stone."

His hand tightened over hers at the mention of the stone. "A piece of flying rock from that thing might have killed you. You were lucky to get off with just a cut. It was the sound of the stone shattering that woke us all."

"Is it damaged badly?"

"The inscription's blasted . . . I didn't really stop to look."

She leaned her head against the cushion and looked through the dining-room door. The table obliterated her view of the window. "The stone saved me, Tom. It turned back the rage. For the first time in my life, I prayed."

There was expectancy in the grim lines of his face and his fine gray eyes. She knew he would not ask her: he would rather have her rest now. His tenderness was unalloyed with impulsiveness or demand. Smiling faintly, she drew in her breath and began the story, telling him everything that had happened from the time she left her room, painting for him all the transformations of Trograin, until the cold came down and the smell, and the stone was blasted. When she finished, his frown was deeper than ever.

"He was mad, darling," she said. "That's why

the festival was called the rage of Trograin. I suspect it included human sacrifice to slake his lust for blood. As a young man, he loved a woman and lost her. Whether she belonged to him in the first place isn't clear. The rest of the story came to me just as the cold came down again. In the battle to regain her . . . or take her . . . he was horribly maimed and disfigured. It affected his mind. His own people killed him . . . in a ritual murder of some sort. We'll have to look this up . . . we don't have Mr. Hughes to help us now. But that's what I saw."

"Only he didn't stay killed."

"No. His hatred was stronger than death. The people probably got so frightened by his forays that they made a god out of him . . . and supplied him victims yearly."

"Love and hate," he pondered, stroking her fingers. "They shouldn't be combined. In one of his forms, he was full of affection. In another, he was destruction itself."

"Of course, none of this can be written into our report. It wouldn't be scientific to report it."

"Why not? We're not going to spend our time turning cards in a lab. We're going to try to get to the bottom of things."

"I want to see the stone."

He did not argue. He wrapped the afghan around her and lifted her in his arms.

"You're strong," she said, surprised.

"I'll have to be," he said, ducking through the door and carrying her into the dining room, "considering the competition. Those fine, naked shoulders . . . I wonder if ghosts ever wear clothes?"

"You read the account I wrote," she said, beginning to struggle.

"Account? Oh. No, I haven't had time to. But maybe I'd better."

He put her down in front of the stone and they stood back to survey the damage. The great mossy boulder was intact, except for the inscription. The remaining letters were blackened as though they had been struck by lightning. The rest of the inscription was gone. A large star-shaped hole disfigured the stone, through which unweathered, living granite showed. Monica removed a few fragments of chipped rock and sadly began to polish the remaining letters with a corner of the afghan. She was so preoccupied with these activities that it was Tom who noticed it first.

"That's curious," he said.

As the first light of day fell on the green moss, she read:

The stone of the Sepulcher.